THE FLOODS

9

Who Wants To Be A Billionaire?

Colin Thompson

illustrations by the author

RANDOM HOUSE AUSTRALIA

This work is fictitious. Any resemblance to anyone living or dead is purely coincidental except for my brother Spruce who is an even bigger idiot than my cousin Crawford.

A Random House book
Published by Random House Australia Pty Ltd
Level 3, 100 Pacific Highway, North Sydney NSW 2060
www.randomhouse.com.au

First published by Random House Australia in 2010

Copyright © Colin Thompson 2010
http://www.colinthompson.com

Addresses for companies within the Random House Group can be found at www.randomhouse.com.au/offices.

National Library of Australia
Cataloguing-in-Publication Entry

Author: Thompson, Colin (Colin Edward)
Title: Who wants to be a billionaire / Colin Thompson
ISBN: 978 1 86471 945 1 (pbk.)
Series: Thompson, Colin (Colin Edward) Floods; 9
Target Audience: For primary school age
Dewey Number: A823.3

Design, illustration and typesetting by Colin Thompson
Additional typesetting by Anna Warren, Warren Ventures Pty Ltd
Printed and bound by Griffin Press

11 10 9 8 7 6 5

THE FLOODS
9

Who Wants To Be A Billionaire?

The Floods Family Tree

KING
MERLIN
Wizard

QUEEN
MORDONNA
Witch

PRINCE
Valla ♥ ### PRINCESS
Mildred

PRINCESS
Satanella

PRINCISH
Merlinmary

PRINCE
Winchflat ♥ ### PRINCESS
Maldegard

PRINCES
Morbid & Silent

PRINCESS
Betty

Now that Winchflat and Valla are married, there are also several pocket versions of princes and princesses known as children. They have not been added to this family tree in case they turn into boiled eggs, which happens a lot to baby wizards under the age of three.

Prologue

Prologues are bits at the beginning of a book that tell you what happened in the earlier books in a series.

They are nearly always very boring and statistics show that only 1.37 per cent of people ever read them. So if you think I'm going to go through the eight books before this one and write a summary of all the incredible things that happened for 1.37 per cent of you, then you've got another thought coming, and that thought should be, *Ooh, I must rush out straight away and get all the other Floods books that I have been too much of a loser to read before.*

But there are two pages here for a prologue so here is a pro log.

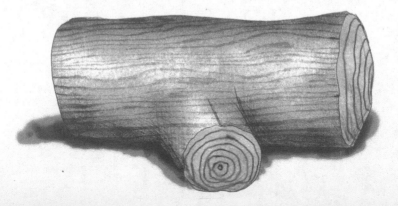

And here is an amateur log.

Now read on . . .

The trouble with living happily ever after is that it can get pretty boring, and for witches and wizards it can get ten times more boring than it does for ordinary people because they are ten times more intelligent than ordinary people.

Ordinary people who are older than about twenty are quite often already on the slippery slope downhill to a life of total boredom, but they pretend they're not by gardening or going on holiday or restoring rusty old cars until they are shining like new, but just as rubbish as they were when they were new because they were rubbish cars in the first place.

Ordinary people who are younger than about

twenty, and know in their hearts that it's only a matter of time until they pass twenty and their lives become boring too, try to pretend it's not happening by sitting in dark places sending hundred of text messages to people who are sitting in a different dark place sending hundreds of text messages all of which say nothing at all, lol, thnx, omg, booms.[1]

There are millions of things humans can do to stop being bored – the trouble is that most of them are even more boring than being bored.

---

[1] *booms = bored out of my skull.*

4

Witches and wizards can do all that stuff in the blink of an eye and a lot more besides. They are too intelligent to spend months putting a cheap, rubbish car back together. All they have to do is a couple of quick spells and what was once a pile of rusty old tin cans in a puddle is suddenly three 1961 Ferrari 250 GT SWB California Spyders.[2] Even simple distractions can be boring. If a wizard want a Cornetto, he doesn't have to drive down to the shops in one of his 1961 Ferrari 250 GT SWB California Spyders. He just clicks his fingers and there's chocolate running down his fingers before you can say, 'I wonder if it's raining in Belgium?'

If a wizard is sitting by a lovely lake and watching the flying jellyfish splattering themselves against the rocks has got boring, he can create an instant island with trees and purple grass and Belgian nudists

---

[2] *A 1961 Ferrari 250 GT SWB California Spyder is the most expensive car ever sold. In an auction someone paid US$10,976,000 for one. Nerlin has five of them, each one an exciting, yet intriguingly different, shade of red to go with whatever mood he is in that day. If he isn't in a red mood, another spell changes the car to the colour of his current mood.*

getting attacked by man-eating thistles. Nerlin Flood, the King of Transylvania Waters, has created seventeen of these islands, though he did make the grass a different colour and the nudists a different nationality on each one. His wife, the sensationally irresistible Queen Mordonna, also created seventeen islands, but hers floated fifty metres above the ground and the nudists all wore clothes so as not to frighten little children as they drifted over their school playgrounds.[3]

Of course, it's hard to imagine that anyone living in a country as staggeringly beautiful as Transylvania Waters, with its exciting furniture-rotting dampness, gorgeous baby-eating plants and vampire kittens, could ever be bored. Most people would give their right arms to live there and in fact

---

[3] *It was the islands, not the little children, who were drifting over the playgrounds. Except, of course, on April the 18th, which is National Drifting Over Playgrounds Day, when everyone in Transylvania Waters floats about. And actually only sixteen of Mordonna's islands drift over the countryside as one of them has got stuck on the spire of Transylvania Waters's one and only church, St Clympna's.*

many people have.[4] There is a small village on the far side of Lake Tarnish where everyone living there has done that, and hidden behind the village in the Big Forest is a colony of immigrants who have sacrificed their eye-teeth too.

It is even harder to imagine that someone who was not only a witch or wizard, but a royal prince or princess too, would ever want to leave this paradise on earth, where magic rocks ooze blood that tastes like nectar and tiny chocolate-flavoured frogs leap

---

[4] *When some of these people were discovered to be left-handed they were deported to Belgium.*

into your mouth to send your taste buds into a frenzy of sheer delight.

But this is exactly what happened. Even though it had only been a short time since the Floods had returned to Transylvania Waters as its rightful rulers, there are times when ruling a country that can only be described as Paradise[5] can get a little boring.

'We hate to admit it,' said the Flood twins Prince Morbid and Prince Silent in the first week of the summer holidays, 'because it sounds very ungrateful, but we're bored.'

'Bored?' said Nerlin. 'How on earth can you be bored? What about the magic rocks that ooze blood and the chocolate-flavoured frogs?'

'Boring,' said Silent, who had begun talking once the family had gone to live in Transylvania Waters.

'And what about school?' said Mordonna.

'Love school,' said Morbid. 'But there's eight weeks until the next term starts.'

---

[5] *Actually, there are lots of ways to describe Transylvania Waters, including 'that weird place where all the witches and wizards live'.*

'What about summer camp?' said Mordonna. 'That might be fun.'

'You have to be kidding,' said Satanella. 'Stuck in the middle of the country with a bunch of goody-goody human nerds, singing camp-fire songs and sleeping in tents? I'd rather eat my own feet.'

'Ah, no,' said Mordonna. 'Not human summer camp. Quicklime College[6] Summer School. The brochure arrived this morning.'

'What, stuck in the middle of the country with a bunch of junior wizards, singing camp-fire songs and sleeping in tents?' said the twins. 'We've only got to look out of the window to see the country already, this place is full of it. And we hate singing.'

'Yes, and as you know,' Merlinmary added, 'camping is illegal in Transylvania Waters.'[7]

'No, no, it's nothing like that,' said Mordonna.

---

[6] *If you want to find out all about Quicklime College, then read* The Floods 2: Playschool. *In fact, if you haven't read it, then put this book down and rush out and get it now so I don't have to keep repeating myself telling you who everyone is.*

[7] *The reason camping is illegal in Transylvania Waters is because they have the sense to realise that sleeping in a bag on*

'For a start it's in New York, no trees, no tents, no grass and all that nature stuff. Quicklime's Summer School is in a block of luxury apartments in Manhattan.'

'No sleeping bags?'

'King-size beds in every room,' said Mordonna.

'No cooking lumps of flour and water on a stick in a bonfire?'[8]

'Luxury German kitchens on every floor, it says here,' said Mordonna, holding up the brochure. 'With servants to clean for you. Servants who were trained by the finest British Butler School, it says.'

'That sounds OK,' said Satanella, 'but what are we supposed to do all day? I can't see rock climbing or traversing ravines or white water rafting happening much in New York.'

---

lumpy ground under a thin bit of leaky canvas is not so much a holiday as a very cruel type of punishment.

[8] *Which is what we had to do at Scout Camp. It has proved invaluable because I've lost count of the number of times I've been stranded somewhere with nothing but some flour, some water, a bonfire and a stick and wondered what to have for dinner. Without that training I would probably eat the stick.*

'You will have many exciting opportunities to put all the things you have learnt at school into practice,' Mordonna read out.

'Now that could have endless possibilities,' said Winchflat.

'Winchflat, I think we need to talk about you and school,' said Mordonna. 'I mean, you're married and have a daughter now. Don't you think it's time you left school?'

'We'll talk about that when we get back from New York,' said Winchflat. 'I've got some inventions I want to try and that will be the perfect place.'

Mordonna and Nerlin knew better than to ask Winchflat what the inventions were. Although they all spoke the same language, once Winchflat started explaining what one of his gadgets was and how it worked, it was as if he was talking Belgian and they came from Paraguay or Mars. They also knew that telling him to make sure none of his gadgets broke the law was pointless, because every one of his inventions was always fitted with a Change-The-Law-So-It's-All-Legal-Attachment that meant he could get away with murder, not that murder was something he had ever considered. When you are a wizard with awesome powers like Winchflat, there are far more creative ways of dealing with evil people than murder.

So it was decided that apart from Valla, who was a bit busy doing government stuff, and baby Charlie Hulbert, who was busy just doing stuff,[9] all the Flood children and Ffiona Hulbert would go to Quicklime College Summer School.

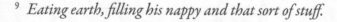

---

[9] *Eating earth, filling his nappy and that sort of stuff.*

The Quicklime College Summer School was held in a beautiful old apartment block right in the heart of Manhattan. Until the day before there had been a lot of extremely rich families living in the beautiful spacious apartments, but they had all decided very suddenly that they wanted to live in other places and every one of them had sold their apartments to the same property company who, by an amazing coincidence, just happened to have set up office on the ground floor of the building. They paid each owner quite a lot more than they had ever imagined their apartments were worth and found them all new places to live at bargain basement prices and even moved their furniture for them with their own fleet of removal vans. So everyone was happy. That night a firm of Transylvania Waters interior decorators had completely remodelled the entire building, fitting it out with all the things a wizard summer school could ever need, from soundproof rooms to a five-star cafeteria. The penthouse suite on the top floor, which had wonderful views out across the city, was converted into one huge room where all the staff and students could meet.

When the students, staff and teachers had arrived from their various homes around the world, the Headmaster, Professor Throat, gathered them all together in the penthouse.

'Look out there, boys and girls,' he said, pointing to the streets below. 'That is the biggest bag of money in the world.'

Many of the staff and teachers from Quicklime College had come to the school too. The Cook was particularly excited at the opportunity to play with all the new hi-tech cooking gadgets that had been installed. Back at the school in Patagonia the latest

14

cooking implement was a wooden spoon that had once been used by King Henry VIII of England to dig the wax out of his ears. Sure, it gave the soup a unique flavour, but now the Cook could play with microwaves – she never lost the thrill of watching a hen's egg explode as she turned the power up to maximum.[10] She even had one of the latest steam ovens at her disposal, which proved wonderful for shrinking baggy knickers.

'Excuse me, Headmaster,' said Aubergine Wealth, the economics teacher, 'but I think you'll find that New York is only the second biggest bag. The biggest bag of money is called Switzerland.'[11]

'Oh dear,' said the Headmaster. 'Do you think

---

[10] *WARNING: Do NOT try this at home, or outdoors or in anyone else's home, and NEVER try it while the egg is still inside the chicken – which the Cook was tempted to, but DIDN'T.*

[11] *What Aubergine Wealth didn't say was that Wall Street was probably the third biggest bag of money because his own bag of money, which he kept under his bed, was actually bigger. Yes, he had a VERY BIG bed and 'under his bed' was actually seven stories of his house, which were all packed to their ceilings with cash, jewellery, bonds, and metals and diamonds.*

15

we should have set up Summer School there then? After all, as we pointed out in the Summer School brochure, our reason for being here is to screw up the banking systems and make as much money as we possibly can.'

'Absolutely not, Headmaster,' said the Cook. 'The food in Switzerland is really boring.'

Aubergine Wealth most certainly didn't want the school to be in Switzerland. That was where he had more of his immense fortune hidden away. The last thing he wanted was a bunch of junior wizards poking around in all those lovely Swiss banks.

'Zee people are really boring too, sir,' said a small boy called Valter Varnish, the last of a very rare breed – Swiss Wizards. 'Zis I know because I live zere.'

'Fair enough,' said the Headmaster. 'We'll start in New York, then.'

'So what are we going to do, exactly?' said Betty. 'I mean, Summer School usually involves all sorts of healthy activities like hiking and learning to tie useless knots.'

'Both of which will be very useful here,' said the Headmaster. 'We'll be hiking over the road to the Stock Exchange and tying the whole thing up in knots while we quietly take over. This may all seem new to you, but I'll hand over to Professor Wealth, who will explain that this is actually something we have been working on for quite some time.'

'Indeed and thank you, Headmaster,' said Aubergine Wealth. 'I'm sure most of you know that the world's financial markets are in a terrible state and it appeared to happen almost overnight. Well, of course, it didn't.'[12]

'The Summer School Project,' Aubergine continued, 'is for every student to make as much money as they possibly can. Students can work in

---

[12] *We have a problem here and it's this: most intelligent people fall asleep when someone starts talking about stocks and shares and accounts and sub-prime mortgages. I know I do. And why? Because it's REALLY, REALLY BORING. After all, there is only one thing you need to know – always try to get more money than you are spending. The trouble is that this story is all about sub-pr . . .*

Oops, sorry, fell asleep there.

groups or individually and pretty well anything is fair game – buy and sell, wheel and deal, and try to stay within the law though it's not essential. I think we all agree it sounds a lot more exciting than hiking through mud and weaving grass into comfortable bedding.'

'When Mr Wealth says there are no rules,' said the Headmaster, 'he only means as far as making money is concerned. All the standard Quicklime Rules, such as taking flying broomsticks home at weekends, apply here the same as they do at school. Though you are not encouraged to rob little old ladies.'

'Unless they are nasty little old ladies, then you can take them for everything they've got,' said Aubergine.

'Absolutely,' agreed the Headmaster.

'And remember, children,' said Quicklime's Matron, 'that I am here to treat you in case the old ladies hit back. Some of them are pretty dangerous. They can take your eyes out with a well-aimed handbag.'

The first thing the students had to do was disguise themselves, because the Stock Exchange wouldn't let anyone younger than eighteen inside. Once again Winchflat came to the rescue with some wonderful I-May-Look-Too-Young-But-Here-Is-My-Driving-Licence-Which-Tells-You-I-Am-Twenty-One-Hats. Whoever wore one, even if they were eight or eighty-eight years old, instantly made any human believe they were twenty-three and old enough for anything.

The Cook, who was fifty-seven, put one on and went downstairs to the nearest bar where seven twenty-two-year-old yuppies fell in love with her.

As well as the magic hats, everyone was given a disguise. All the girls were turned blonde, with big, powerful hairstyles because it is against regulations for women to enter the New York Stock Exchange if they are not blonde. There is actually a special doorman whose sole job is to check female blondeness. If there is a hint of any other colour in their hair or the style is not big enough, they are banned. One of the most successful shops in New York is a hairdressers opposite the Exchange that specialises in blonding and plumping up. It's called 'Who Wants To Have A Million Hairs?'[13]

Capes, pointed hats and all the other lovely clothes witches and wizards wear were replaced with boring business suits, flashy waistcoats and clipboards.

'Excellent,' said Aubergine Wealth as he inspected his students. 'Let's go to work.'

'Excuse me, sir,' said Betty, 'but what exactly are we going to do?'

'We are going to take over the world.'

'Fair enough,' said Betty. 'How?'

---

[13] *One of the most popular souvenirs you can buy in New York is the special New York Stock Exchange Barbie Doll, which has twice as much blonde hair as any other Barbie.*

'We are going to buy everything,' said Aubergine Wealth. 'Or rather, everything that's valuable.'

'All of the sticks?' said Satanella. 'Wow, and can we buy all the red rubber balls too?'

'Sticks, what sticks?' said Aubergine Wealth.

'On the Stick Exchange,' said Satanella.

'It's the Stock Exchange,' said Aubergine Wealth.

'Now that's where I come in,' said the Cook. 'If there's one thing I know a lot about it's stock – chicken stock, beef stock, lizard stock, you name it. I've got recipes for them all.'

Aubergine Wealth sat down and buried his head in his hands.

'Well, I do,' said the Cook.

'No doubt, dear lady,' said Aubergine Wealth. 'But they're not that sort of stocks.'

'Don't worry, dear,' said the Cook. 'I've used them all, even Tasmanian tiger and dodo and cabbage. If a stock exists, I've made it.'

Aubergine Wealth groaned. This sort of thing is a common problem for anyone who is an expert on

something that might look a bit complicated, such as building a nuclear-powered spaceship or making soy products actually taste half-decent. Experts who can perform advanced quadratic equations[14] in their sleep whilst reciting π to nineteen million places simply can't get their heads round the fact that there are people for whom adding one and one is a foreign country they will never visit.

So it was that, after Aubergine Wealth had recovered from explaining stocks to the Cook and finished describing Naked Short Selling,[15] most of them thought it meant taking your trousers off and selling them. Of course, Winchflat and the three-legged Maranzio triplets from the Isle of Man[16] understood straightaway. So it was decided that the four of them would go to the Stock Exchange and

---

[14] *I don't know what they are, but they sound really complicated and BORING.*

[15] *I don't know what that is either, but I do know that it's illegal. Probably better if you look this up on Google.*

[16] *Which I believe is about to be re-named the Isle of Non-Specific-Gender Persons because of a European Commission on Equality regulation.*

start wheeling and dealing while the other children would do the things they were best at.

'So, at the end of each day, we will all meet back here,' said the Headmaster, 'and whoever has made the most money at the end of Summer School will get a prize.'

'But, aren't there more important things in life than money?' said Betty.

The room fell silent. Everyone, including Ffiona, was speechless.

'Wow,' said Merlinmary finally. 'Our little sister has turned into a hippy.'

3

As you know, it's a different time of day in different parts of the world. Although this makes life quite complicated, it's not nearly as complicated as it would be if it was the same time everywhere. If it was, we would have to go to bed before breakfast and eat dinner in our sleep and *Desperate Housewives* would finish before it had started.

When work finishes for the day in one country and banks and stock exchanges close for the night, it is just beginning in another and some people make lots of money simply by moving it around the world. If what they are doing is against the law in one country, all they have to do is move to a different country where it isn't. Transylvania Waters is probably the best country in the world to be if you want to get as rich as possible as quickly as possible without getting into trouble. Most countries have a business district where most of the banks and stocks and shares places are. Transylvania Waters has one too, but because the country is run by witches and wizards, theirs is better. On one side of the street it is always five minutes before the end of the working day no matter what country you are dealing with. And on the other side of the street it is five minutes after work starts. Just by walking over the road, you can have someone's money to play with for a whole day, before they expect it to arrive, and if you do this on a Friday, their money is yours for a whole weekend.

When it comes to horse-racing, time is very important too. Obviously, you are only allowed to place a bet before a race starts. But if you are a witch or a wizard that's not a problem – and if you are an identical twin as well, you can't fail.

While Morbid went to the biggest bookmakers in New York, Silent went to the race track to choose the horses. Five minutes before the race was to start, Morbid made every single clock and watch in the whole of New York go back two-and-a-half minutes, except for the starter's. Silent noted the winners of each race and sent them telepathically to Morbid, who then placed a bet.

Obviously, if he had bet on every race, it would have looked a bit suspicious. So he only chose the races where an outsider, who wasn't expected to win and therefore offered much better odds, had won. After a couple of races, Morbid went to a different bookmaker and placed his winnings on another race. At some point between races, when he calculated no one would notice, he changed the clocks back to the right time.

Humans had tried this sort of thing themselves, but had always got found out. One at the race track talked to one in the betting shop with a walkie-talkie. Of course, humans couldn't make all the clocks jump backwards and forwards like Morbid so they seldom managed to place a bet in time. The twins also had extra insurance. If anyone ever became suspicious and looked at the security camera records from the race track and the betting shops, they would see what looked like the same person in the same place at the same time, which is impossible.[17]

'It's like taking candy from a baby,' Morbid said at the end of the day as the twins counted out the money they had won.

One million, six hundred and thirty-four thousand dollars.

They were at the top of the leader board.

---

[17] *TRUE STORY: A little while ago a man was arrested for speeding in Germany. He claimed his identical brother had been driving the car and because the police could not prove beyond any doubt which twin had been driving, he got away with it!*

At the bottom of the leader board was Betty, who still thought it was all a bit wrong. She had made seven dollars and fifty cents selling lemonade in the street on the coldest day of the month when everyone really wanted a hot drink and had only bought the lemonade because they felt sorry for her. Even Ffiona had made more than Betty just by taking empty bottles she picked up round the streets to the recycling centre.

'There must be some way to make a lot of money

that isn't bad,' said Ffiona, who quite liked the idea of being rich.

'What, you mean like Robin Hood, taking from the rich to give to the poor?' said Betty.

'Yes, that would be OK, sort of,' said Ffiona.

'What do you mean, sort of?'

'Well, as long as the poor was us. I mean, I never really believed Robin Hood. After all, he was an English Lord, so he was probably rich anyway,' said Ffiona. 'I don't think his giving to the poor involved giving them any of his own money. If he'd really been such a great, kind, lovely person, he could have just given his own money away and not bothered with all the robbing and stuff.'

'What's your idea then?' said Betty.

'Well, I like the robbing from the rich bit,' Ffiona said. 'It's the giving it away bit I don't like.'

'So, you think we should rob from the rich and keep it?'

'Yes,' said Ffiona, but seeing Betty was not so keen she added, 'We needn't keep all of it.'

'I suppose that wouldn't be so bad,' said Betty.

'We rob from the rich, keep some of it and give some of it away?'

'Well, not exactly.'

'What exactly then?'

'Well, we steal from the rich, keep some of it and then go shopping,' said Ffiona.

'Oh, I see, buy stuff to give to the poor like food and clothes and things they haven't got?'

'No,' said Ffiona. 'We buy stuff that we haven't got like designer clothes and PlayStations and nice shoes.'

'I think that's probably bad.'

'Not for us,' said Ffiona. 'And we could have brilliant highwayman costumes with, like, black velvet masks with diamonds on, and big leather boots.'

'And horses?' said Betty, who was maybe, perhaps, possibly, beginning to warm to the idea. 'Could we have horses?'

'Could do,' said Ffiona, 'though I think I'd favour high-speed motorbikes, but we could use horses in Central Park or if we go out to the country.'

'Have you got any pictures of the black velvet masks?'

'I have, actually.'

So it was decided. The two girls would become highwaymen, or rather, highwaywomen or, to be even more accurate, highwaygirls, which sounded rubbish, so they agreed to stick with highwaymen.

Unlike the twins, who started their betting with five dollars, and Winchflat and the Maranzio triplets, who started their share dealing with some creative lies, Betty and Ffiona's project required a much larger investment, and as each student had only been given fifty dollars to start with, they instantly ran into a problem.

'Do you know how much a horse costs in New York?' said Betty. 'It's ridiculous. They're way more expensive than motorbikes and we haven't got enough to buy a bicycle. I mean, even a couple of black velvet masks will cost more than we've got.'

'Where there's a will there's a way,' said Ffiona. 'Obviously the first things we need to steal from the rich are horses, motorbikes and black velvet masks.'

'There are horses in Central Park,' said Betty. 'You can have a ride in a horse-drawn carriage and there are policemen on horseback too.'

Central Park was a long way from the Summer School campus, too far to walk, so the girls decided to steal a motorbike. That created another problem.

'Do you know how to drive a motorbike?' said Ffiona.

'Not as such, but I do know how to drive a flying broomstick,' said Betty. 'It can't be that different.'

One of the rules of Summer School was that no students were allowed to take flying broomsticks. There had been protests from students and parents. After all, broomsticks are super environmentally friendly. The resources they use up are one stick, a bundle of twigs and a bit of string, and they don't need any fuel to run. But they were banned in New York because it was decided the sight of children flying around the city on brooms would totally freak out the human population and probably cause a lot of accidents with people driving their cars into things and people walking into signposts.

'Not to mention all the dogs trying to run away with them, like they did when we had that school trip to Paris last year,' the Headmaster had said. 'There are still three poodles missing who grabbed hold of them and were carried off into the clouds before their owners could call them back.'

After they had watched a few motorbikes drive past, the girls decided that maybe it was not quite the same as flying a broom.

'OK then,' said Ffiona, 'why don't we start with the black velvet masks? They can't be difficult to get.'

But compared to Transylvania Waters, New York is useless for shopping. As incredible as it may seem, there is not a single branch of DisGuys'n'Gals, where you can buy everything the well-dressed witch or wizard would want to wear from pointy hats to turbo wands.[18] In fact, a search of several blocks failed to turn up a single shop where you could buy even a simple black velvet mask.

---

[18] *See the back of this book for some of the more popular and fashionable items on sale there.*

34

That night Betty and Ffiona were still at the bottom of the list. They had spent the entire day on their highwayman plans and hadn't actually made a single cent between them, apart from the single cent

Ffiona had picked up in the gutter. The twins, on the other hand, had another great day at the races and made another million-plus dollars.

The two girls were too embarrassed to tell anyone what they'd been doing. In Transylvania Waters even a two-year-old could find a black velvet mask. So if they'd told anyone, they'd have been a laughing-stock.

The next morning they crept out of the building before anyone else was up. Over a bowl of porridge in Auntie Crab's Greasy Spoon Diner down an alley across the street, they decided what to do next.

'What is a mask for?' said Ffiona.

'To hide your face, so no one can tell who you are,' said Betty.

'Exactly, and we can't find any, can we?'

'So what are you suggesting?'

'Improvisation,' said Ffiona.

Ffiona took a thick black texta out of her pocket and drew a mask on Betty's face.[19] She then

---

[19] *You know how it always says in books, 'Don't try this at home'? Well, this is different. I think you SHOULD try this at*

handed the pen to Betty to do the same for her. This would not have fooled anyone who knew them for an instant, but they were not going to rob people they knew.

'This whole disguise thing a bit pointless,' said Betty. 'In fact, it's actually the opposite of a disguise.'

'How?' said Ffiona.

'Well, if people we've robbed go to the police and the police ask them what we looked like and they say, "They had pretend masks drawn on their faces," as soon as we set foot outside looking like this we'll be arrested,' said Betty. 'We're certainly going to be the only two children in New York looking like that.'

'Good point,' said Ffiona. 'But if we weren't the only two, then it would be a brilliant disguise.'

'Meaning?'

'What if all the children the same age as us had black masks drawn on their faces?'

---

home. I think the world would be a better place if lots and lots of you drew black masks on your faces. See the back of the book for instructions.

'How on earth are we going to do that?' said Betty.

'Duh, you're a witch, remember,' said Ffiona. 'You can do magic spells. Couldn't you make a spell so every kid wakes up tomorrow with a black mask?'

'Yes, of course. Brilliant,' said Betty.

'Why didn't you just use magic to give us masks,' said Ffiona, 'instead of us having to muck about with textas?'

'You know my magic sort of doesn't always come out exactly how I plan,' Betty explained. 'When I was little I tried to make a Hello Kitty mask appear on my face and I ended up with a bright ginger beard. Which I can tell you is not a good look for a five-year-old, boy or girl. Mum was furious and made me keep it for a month before she magicked it away. Dad was even more cross because I kept using his razor and made it go all blunt.'

'You don't think all the children in New York will get ginger beards, do you?' said Ffiona.

'Who knows?' said Betty. 'Be a bit of a laugh if they did, wouldn't it?'

38

Although Betty was a witch and could do magic, most of her spells didn't come out exactly as she planned.[20] She had once turned a small boy into a big fridge when all she had intended to do was give him a fright. On that occasion the result had been a good one. The boy had been vile and made a far better contribution to society as a fridge than he ever would have done as a human.

This time, however, no one was delighted at the outcome.

The next morning, every single child in New York woke up with a mask. The masks were not black but bright red like super-neon luminous tomatoes. That alone wouldn't have been a problem. The two girls could simply have repainted their mask to match. No, the problem was where the mask had appeared. They were not covering the top half of their faces, but splashed across every child's bottom.

'I don't know what all the fuss is about,' said Betty after she had Ffiona had re-coloured their

---

own masks red. 'At least they're not all hairy.'

Mothers across New York panicked and traffic came to a total stop as they tried to drive their much-too-big cars with their screaming children in the back to the nearest hospital. The city was thrown into complete chaos.

The children were not in any pain, but it did appear that the red mask-shaped patches on their bottoms were growing bigger and bigger and a rumour ran round the city that once the two halves of mask met and joined up, you would die. This, of course, was complete rubbish and all everyone would have had to do was wait for a few days until the marks began to fade away. But at the time, no one, not even Betty, knew that and panic spreads very quickly nowadays with newspapers and television all desperate to grab the headlines by turning a simple cold into a plague that is threatening to wipe out the whole world in fourteen minutes.

Nobody can get a simple cold or a dose of the flu any more. People get struck down with Goldfish-

flu or the terrible vegetarian illness called Toflu. If you catch Vegetarian Toflu, you become terminally smug and everyone near you is at risk of dying of boredom. One sneeze these days and everyone expects tens of thousands of people to drop dead from a new and much-deadlier-than-the-last-outbreak-which-was-actually-fairly-harmless virus. If you cough while you're bending down to tie your shoelace and get run over by a car, the newspapers are guaranteed to scream, 'Pandemic Claims Another Victim!!!!'

Schools closed, in case the new mystery disease was catching. Shops and streets were deserted. All the goldfish were flushed down toilets because some idiot said the outbreak was being transferred by them.

'Stands to reason, doesn't it?' said a leading doctor. 'The outbreak manifests itself in bright red weals and goldfish are orange, which is nearly red.'

'Maybe it's being spread by mailboxes,' said a professor of rubbish from some learned institution. 'They're red.'

So everyone panicked for no sensible reason at all and stopped posting letters.

'Oops,' said Betty.

She felt rather guilty so at the Summer School meeting that evening, she admitted what had happened. Instead of getting into trouble, most of the other students and staff thought it was hilarious and went out and committed an enormous amount of highway robbery by disguising themselves as health officials with fake Red Plague Scanners and telling all the distressed mothers that they had located the germs and would have to remove the source immediately in order to irradiate it and kill the germs before they spread.

Amazingly, the source was always inside handbags, particularly in the wallet area.

'Humans are so pathetic,' said the Headmaster. 'Why, I have had the bubonic plague for the past twenty-three years and it's never done me any harm.'

'It's not like this is causing any real harm, either,' said the Matron. 'I remember a similar outbreak in Scotland many years ago when everyone's arms turned tartan.'

'My favourite one was in 1987,' said the Cook. 'The one in Belgium when everyone's legs turned back to front. If I remember rightly that was caused by one of the Floods too.'

'Do you mean that I'm not the only one who has magic go wrong?' said Betty.

'Oh no,' said the Matron. 'Your family's famous for it. Happens in all top wizard families. And after all, your father is King of our beloved Transylvania Waters. You don't get much topper than that. The Belgian leg affair happened when your Great-Aunt Florinse tried to turn a ginger kitten into a tabby.'

'No one ever told me that,' said Betty. 'It would have been reassuring to know I inherited Clumsy Magic.'

'But coming back to our current problem,' said the Headmaster, 'we need to discuss the situation. And by discuss, I mean, of course, work out all the ways we can profit from it.'

Matron nodded. 'My previous experiences of bright red marks on various parts of the body is that they will probably start to fade in about five days and vanish completely in ten,' she said.

'So we've got about a week,' said the Headmaster.

Some students were already doing very nicely

out of the situation. As racing had been cancelled in case the new Red Plague was catching for horses, the twins and Merlinmary were out on the streets selling Special Anti-Red-Plague Facemasks for twenty-five dollars each, which by a skilful bit of time travel they had made the day before in Taiwan for five cents a dozen. They added dog and cat masks to their range, which Satanella modelled for passersby, and their sales almost doubled.[21] Soya-Vegetarian-Recycled-Toilet-Paper Masks and Kosher Masks increased their sales too.

Once again the twins were top of the money-making list, even after they had given Betty and Ffiona ten per cent commission because they had made all the bottoms go red in the first place. Ffiona and Betty with their commission and the confiscated wallets were a very close second.

---

[21] *There are a huge number of dogs and cats in New York with very devoted owners.*

45

4

The Stock Exchange was almost deserted. It wasn't actually closed, but instead of the hundreds of people who went there every day, only a couple of dozen were there. Betty's Red Plague had only affected people in New York, so all the other stock markets around the world were still working away as normal, though everywhere was on edge in case the plague spread. This made all the stock brokers and bankers very, very cautious. Naturally, Winchflat and Aubergine Wealth were there and made a fortune. All they had to do was buy almost anything, start a simple rumour or two to make the price rocket and sell it few hours later to make millions. With so few people around, there was no one available to check if the rumours were true or not, and with such an air of panic everywhere people tended to believe every single one of them.

'At least all the babies will stop getting fat,' Winchflat laughed.

'I don't follow,' said Aubergine as he stuffed wads of share documents into his pockets.

'Well, today has been like stealing candy from a baby,' Winchflat explained.

'You know what we should do?' said Aubergine Wealth. 'We need to corner something, not something people usually try to corner like gold or silver, but something much simpler that everyone uses and needs every day.'

'You mean, like tea or coffee?' said Winchflat.

'Sort of, but something much more basic and something no one would expect it to happen to.'

To 'corner' the market in something means trying to own as much of it as possible. If you can own all of it, so much the better. For example, supposing

potatoes usually cost twenty cents each and you wanted one. You would go to the shop, hand over twenty cents and get your potato.

Now, supposing you went to the shop and there were no potatoes because someone had bought every single one of them. By now, of course, you are really desperate for a potato, so you go to the person who owns them all and say, 'Can I have a potato?'

Boutique Special $42.00

Family Spud $23.99

SPUD of the WEEK $15.99

'Of course you can,' says the potato baron. 'How many do you want?'

'Two, please,' you say, handing over forty cents.

'What's that?' says the potato king.

'Forty cents, for the two potatoes,' you say.

'Very funny,' says the potato god. 'They cost five dollars each.'

'But . . .'

That is 'cornering' the market.

Winchflat and Aubergine Wealth sat and thought. Potatoes were not a good choice. People could just eat rice or pasta.

'There's no food at all that would work, really,' said Aubergine Wealth.

'Chocolate might,' said Winchflat. 'People would go frantic if they couldn't get a chocolate hit.'

'True, but they might go more than frantic. They might get uncontrollably angry and start rioting,' said Aubergine Wealth. 'Also, not everyone is addicted to chocolate.'

'Are you sure?'

'Yes. We need something very basic that everyone needs, like toilet paper or underwear.'

'Or both.'

'I wasn't serious,' said Aubergine Wealth. 'I didn't actually mean toilet paper or underwear.'

'Think about it,' said Winchflat. 'They are perfect. Everyone uses them. Well, apart from a few strange hippies and rock stars, and we can live without them.'

'You're absolutely right. Which one shall we do first?'

'Toilet paper,' said Winchflat.

One of the weaknesses of trying to own all of something is that lots of people will already have some. Normally not in large quantities, but often enough to see them through any shortage. Every supermarket in the world has shelves full of toilet paper, so most people wouldn't even notice there was a shortage for quite a while.

One of the strengths of trying to own all of something is doing it if you are a wizard with awesome powers. The basement of Quicklime

College's Summer School had been fitted out as a laboratory containing everything a brilliant and enterprising young wizard like Winchflat might need to build absolutely anything he wanted to, no matter how amazing it might be. Winchflat's wife, the disgustingly beautiful Maldegard Ankle, had not come to Summer School. She had far too much to do back in Transylvania Waters.[22] She was, however, in permanent 24/7 contact with her adoring husband as they were both wearing Winchflat's Permanent-24/7-Contact-Socks.

The first thing Winchflat needed was a very large space to put all the toilet rolls he collected with the machine. Luckily Maldegard knew of the perfect spot because one of the too many things she had to do that can be mentioned here was making the first ever really detailed map of Transylvania Waters.[23]

'I have discovered the Caves of Huge Darkness,' she told Winchflat.

---

[22] *Don't ask.*
[23] *See* The Floods 11: Desperate Housewitches.

'Wow,' he said. 'I always thought they were made up, like fairy-story stuff.'

'Well, my darling,' Maldegard replied, 'the whole of Transylvania Waters is such a wonderful and magical place that it's all kind of fairy-story stuff, isn't it?[24]

The Caves of Huge Darkness were originally created by the first wizards to live in Transylvania Waters when they fled there to escape persecution from the Knights Intolerant,[25] who were determined to rid the world of every single wizard and witch by

---

[24] *Maldegard had discovered the entrance to the caves when she had been out searching for Gasper Berries in the deserted dungeons below the cellars below the kitchens of Castle Twilight. She had read about the legendary berries that are the sourest thing in the whole world – one berry is enough to make your mouth shrink smaller than a mosquito's bottom – and gone searching for them in the least likely place they would be, guessing that because no one else had ever found them, that was exactly where they would be. She was the first person in living and half-dead memory to go down to the dungeons and, sure enough, there were berries growing and glowing everywhere. And that was where she had found the tiny door that led into the Caves of Huge Darkness.*

[25] *See* The Floods 7: Top Gear.

the most painful methods possible. The caves were to be the final place to hide if they were ever invaded. However, the Knights Intolerant never managed to reach Transylvania Waters and so the caves were gradually forgotten.

Winchflat had never quite believed the caves

existed, but just to make sure he had built a Big-Hollow-Places-Detector, which told him there was a space beneath Transylvania Waters. It told him it was hollow and it told him it was incredibly big, but didn't tell him where the way in was. Finding the entrance was one of the things near the top of his Must-Do-List, which was stored in his Must-Do-List-Storage-Device, which was like a notebook only different in highly technical and exciting ways that mere humans could never understand. Now his wonderful wife had found it and he looked forward to getting home again so they could both explore it together before they let anyone else know about it.

After all, he thought, *you never know when a big hollow place might come in handy.*

'I know a secret place that will be perfect to hide all the toilet rolls,' he told Aubergine Wealth, though he didn't tell him where it was. 'When we go on to stage two and corner the undies, there will be room for those too.'

Winchflat went to the basement laboratory and designed a massive Toilet-Roll-Magnet-With-

Kitchen-Roll-And-Tissue-Attachments-Machine.

Although he desperately wanted to know where Winchflat was going to hide everything, Aubergine Wealth knew better than to try to force Winchflat to tell him. Although Aubergine was a wizard himself, and there were few his equal when it came to making huge amounts of money, he knew that Winchflat had awesome magical powers he could never compete with. He was, after all, one of the Floods, descended from Merlin, the greatest wizard of all time.

I'll wait, he thought. *The boy will give it away sooner or later.*

Yeah, as if, thought Winchflat, who was wearing his invisible Thought Reader. For some reason he wasn't sure of, instinct told him to tell absolutely no one about the vast cave complex, not even his own family.[26]

While Winchflat was sorting out his machine, Aubergine Wealth went over to the Stock Exchange and began buying shares in every single paper

---

[26] *Great minds think alike, because Maldegard sent him a coded text message at that moment saying exactly the same thing.*

manufacturing company. Within two hours he was in control of the entire world's production. Each company then received an email telling them stop production immediately.

'Are we ready?' said Winchflat as he powered up the Toilet-Roll-Magnet-With-Kitchen-Roll-And-Tissue-Attachments-Machine.

He had warned everyone at Summer School to wear safety helmets as there was no way of predicting all the routes the millions upon millions of toilet rolls from all over the world would take on their way to Winchflat's secret storage facility.

'Excuse me,' said Ffiona. 'I've got a question.'

'I'll just start the machine first,' said Winchflat.

'No, no!' said Ffiona. 'This is a very important question you need to answer before you start the machine.'

'OK, what is it?'

'As I understand it,' Ffiona said, 'your machine is going to transport all the toilet paper in the world to a secret location. Right?'

'Yes,' said Winchflat.

'Every single sheet?'

'Yes.'

'So that will include used toilet paper and paper that is actually being used right at this moment?' said Ffiona.

'Yuk!' said almost everyone.[27]

'Ahh,' said Winchflat. 'Hadn't thought of that. Clever girl.'

There was a delay of about an hour while Winchflat built a filter that excluded toilet paper that wasn't the same pastel colour all over (apart from any pretty patterns that might be printed on it).

'There we go,' he said. 'I've added a No-Poo-Attachment. So I think we're good to go unless anyone else can think of something else I need to do.'

'I can,' said Betty. 'I know wiping your bottom with a newspaper is awful, but won't people just do that, or tear pages out of notebooks?'

---

[27] *We will NOT be naming the person who did not think Yuk.*

57

'Another good point,' said Winchflat.

There was a delay of another hour while Winchflat built a Ruff'nit Machine. It was programmed to cut in about thirty seconds after the main machine started and make all the remaining paper in the world Very Itchy.

'You know,' said the Headmaster, 'the business possibilities are endless. I mean, you could make the remaining paper give anyone who used it a rash that could only be cured with a special ointment from a company that we own most of the shares in.'

In the end, it was decided that was probably going a bit far so it was agreed the Ruff'nit Machine would just give anyone who used it a red bottom like Betty's spell had done. It would scare the living daylights out of everyone, but not actually do them any harm.

'You know what might be fun?' said Merlinmary. 'If you made all the bank notes as soft as velvet. Don't you just love the idea of everyone wiping their bottoms with money?'

'It's a bit mean, isn't it?' said Betty.

'It is,' said Merlinmary, 'but also hilarious.'

'But that's sacrilege!' said Aubergine Wealth, who adored money.

'Right,' said Winchflat, 'I think this time we are good to go unless anyone else can think of something else I need to do.'

No one could. So they all put their crash helmets on and Winchflat pressed the Big Brown Button on the front of his machine. At first, it seemed as if nothing was happening, but then toilet rolls began to appear as if out of thin air. It was incredible, but the soft rolls of paper were actually moving through solid walls before flying off down the streets and out to sea.

Roll after roll appeared, mixed up with loose sheets of paper and packets of tissues. There were so many of them it looked like a snow storm as they flew out of shops and offices and bathrooms and people's hands all over the world. It also cleared all the finished paper out of the factories that Aubergine Wealth had bought the shares in. Small clouds of paper merged into bigger clouds, some of them over a mile wide. Tracking stations around the world picked up the tissue clouds and followed them out into the middle of every ocean. And then, they all suddenly vanished.

Winchflat knew they would be picked up by radar and there was no way he wanted anyone to know where they were going. So, once the paper clouds had grown as large as they were going to, he pressed Button B and they dematerialised into individual atoms too small to follow and continued their journey. Once they reached the Caves of Huge Darkness, all the atoms joined up again and the toilet rolls, tissues and other soft papers collected in piles over the cave floor, where an ancient relic from the age of dinosaurs – the Complaining

Woodlouse,[28] a sort of blind beetle the size of a shoe – began to eat them.

From the inside of millions of bathrooms everywhere came horrified and disgusted screams from people who had been too close to using their handful of toilet paper to stop.[29] The noise was deafening. Apart from the screams, there were hundreds of thousands of people calling out for their mums,

---

[28] *They probably weren't actually complaining. It's just that their mating calls sounded like they were. So did their singing, snoring and territorial calls. Though of course, if you are the only very small beetle in a world full of dinosaurs with very big clumsy feet, you would complain. I suppose if everyone called you a louse you'd complain too.*

[29] *There had been similar cries from behind bushes, deep in forests and several places where this sort of thing should not have been happening.*

thousands of voices screaming every swear word known to man in every language known to man and woman.[30]

The chaos that occurred that day was endless. People about to blow their noses suddenly sneezed into their own hands or, worse still, someone else's hands. Spilled tea, coffee, blood and red wine just soaked into pale clean carpets, clothes and furniture. Governments around the world accused each other of a terrible plot. No one knew how it had happened,

---

[30] *Have you ever wondered how many people at any given moment are actually going to the lavatory around the world? I know I haven't, but let's work it out.*

There are around six-and-a-half thousand million people in the world. Now if you calculate that going to the lavatory takes about five minutes over the course of a day, and five minutes is point-three-five per cent of a day, then you can say that at any single moment of any single day, point-three-five per cent of the world's population is going to the lavatory. That means there are over twenty-two million people having a poo or a wee at the same time. So if we say that half of them were clutching a handful of toilet paper, that is eleven million screaming people – probably the loudest noise ever heard on earth. Makes you think, doesn't it? Actually, it probably makes you wish you could stop thinking.

but the Russians blamed the Chinese. The Chinese blamed the Japanese. The Japanese blamed the Indians. The Indians blamed the British and the Americans blamed everyone.

Only Tristan da Cunha didn't blame anyone because none of their toilet paper had disappeared. Winchflat had a soft spot for Tristan da Cunha and had added a special filter that excluded them. Naturally Transylvania Waters itself and the Transylvania Waters Summer School's supply of soft, gently scented tissue remained untouched too. But everywhere else, from royal palaces to humble cottages, was totally one hundred per cent soft-paperless.

This time the traffic jams were ten times worse than they had been when Red Bottom Plague had broken out. Everything ground to a complete halt as people abandoned their cars and ran to the nearest supermarket to buy toilet paper. Of course, the shelves where the toilet paper should have been were empty. Sneaky people broke into the checkout tills – not to steal the money, but to take the paper rolls the receipts were printed on. But they had vanished too. Humans can never outsmart a wizard.

Enterprising people tried to think laterally, which means thinking sideways to try and find a solution to a problem that is not the usual solution.

This is what they thought.

If there is no paper, what else can we use to wipe our bottoms?

Here are a few things that do not work:

- *Lettuce leaves.*
- *Goldfish.*
- *Sticky tape.*
- *Golf clubs.*
- *Weet-Bix.*

- *Skateboards.*
- *Belgium.*

Here are a few things that do work, though you have to be pretty desperate:

- *Kittens.*
- *Wigs.*
- *Cardigans.*
- *Armchairs.*
- *Seaweed.*
- *Bacon.*
- *Parrots.*
- *Small children.*

Here are some things you must NEVER use:

- *Copies of* The Floods.
- *Dynamite.*
- *Mashed potato.*
- *Belgian dynamite wrapped in barbed wire.*
- *Your baby sister.*

Some people decided they would not go to the toilet until the crisis was over. Some of them exploded.

A few days later posters began to appear everywhere. They were advertising a wonderful new and exciting toilet paper that was softer and fluffier yet much stronger than anything anyone had ever experienced before. The posters said:

CUDDLYCHEEKS

Your bottom will LOVE you so much that you will want to go to the toilet ten times a day.

66

And sure enough, a few days after the posters appeared, all the supermarket shelves were overflowing with Cuddlycheeks. Not only was there toilet paper again, but it really was the softest yet strongest toilet paper that had ever been created.

Everyone was overjoyed.

Until they got to the checkouts.

'Ten dollars a roll!' they cried. 'You must be joking.'

'It's a special introductory offer,' said the checkout girl. 'Next week it goes up to fifteen dollars.'

But everyone paid up. They complained. They argued. They threatened, but they paid up, because if they didn't, there were only too many people who would.

The first week, Transylvania Waters Summer School made three billion dollars.

'This is not so much like taking candy from a baby,' said Professor Throat, 'as taking its toothless gums too.'

The second week, with the price increase, they made six billion dollars. The third week, because

worrying about the high price of toilet paper was making all the humans very stressed, which meant they had to go to the toilet twice as often, they made eight billion dollars.

'I wonder just how much we could get away with charging before people refused to buy it?' said Aubergine Wealth. 'That would be an interesting experiment.'

People were already setting up stalls on street corners and selling toilet paper by the sheet. In the poorer parts of town, shops were being held up at gunpoint by desperate men demanding all the Cuddlycheeks products and people were auctioning sheets on eBay.

The fourth week, the Floods made ten billion dollars.

They knew they could have increased the price to twenty-five dollars a roll, but at twenty dollars a roll, adverts started appearing on the internet and on shop noticeboards offering second-hand toilet paper for sale. That was when they decided it was time to call a stop.

'Except there's still a bit more to be made out of this,' said Aubergine Wealth.

He and Winchflat went to the Stock Exchange and sold all of their shares in all of the paper companies for an outrageously astronomical profit. All, that is, except one small factory in Belgium. The sale did not include the secret recipe for making the ultra-super-soft Cuddlycheeks, but the new owners of the factories didn't care. They just began making the old stuff again. Getting twenty dollars for one roll of toilet paper was fabulous. Money began to pour in like water.

For a whole week.

Then the factory in Belgium began selling Cuddlychecks for fifteen dollars a roll.

'It's OK,' said the new owners of all the other factories. 'We'll charge fourteen dollars a roll. It's still several thousand per cent profit.'

Then the factory in Belgium began selling Cuddlycheeks for ten dollars a roll.

'Oh well, eight dollars a roll is still a huge profit,' said the other factories.

Then the factory in Belgium began selling Cuddlycheeks for five dollars a roll.

'We're still making a profit.'

Then the factory in Belgium began selling Cuddlycheeks for a dollar a roll.

Half the other factories closed down.

Then the factory in Belgium began selling Cuddlycheeks for twenty cents a roll.

The other half of the factories closed down. Aubergine Wealth bought them all back for almost nothing and they all began making Cuddlycheeks and settled on a fair price of two dollars a roll.

By the end of the Great Toilet Roll Enterprise, as it was referred to in Volume Two of Aubergine Wealth's later autobiography, *All Your Monies Are Belong To Me*, the Quicklime College Summer School had made thirty-seven billion dollars.

'I think anything else we do now will be a bit of an anti-climax,' said Professor Throat.

'What about underwear?' said Betty. 'We could do the same thing again with that.'

'What, the same as we did with the toilet paper?' said the Headmaster. 'It's a bit similar, isn't it? The highest marks are not just awarded for the most money, but originality will be taken into account.'

'I think it would be fun,' said Betty. 'All the stuffy uptight people suddenly losing their undies.'

'Now listen, my dear,' said Aubergine Wealth, 'making money is a serious business. It's not something you should think of as fun.'[31]

'Ooh, someone needs to get a life,' said Betty.

'I have a life,' said the economics teacher, 'a very rich, comfortable life actually.'

'Oh yes?' said Betty. 'And your wife and your children, do they have very rich and comfortable lives too?'

'There is no Mrs Wealth. Nor do I have any children.'

'So you live this very rich and comfortable life all on your own, do you?' Betty asked.

---

[31] *Aubergine Wealth had only laughed once in his life and it had been the morning he had opened* The Financial Review *to find that page three had been printed upside-down. He had actually chuckled for twenty-seven seconds and decided as soon as he had finished his breakfast and done the washing up and put the dishes away and made his bed and cleaned his teeth and polished his shoes, he would put his hat and coat on and take the newspaper down to his bank and show it to the bank manager, who he was sure would chuckle too. Sadly this didn't happen because in the two minutes and forty-three seconds he was out of the room, his tortoise, Bullion, ate the newspaper. Naturally, Aubergine Wealth did not waste any money buying another copy. Nothing was that funny.*

'I have a tortoise,' said Aubergine Wealth. 'Bullion.'

'Ooh, I bet it's lovely cuddling up to him on cold winter nights and talking about how your day has been.'

'I do not have cold winter nights. I can afford heating. And yes, I do talk to Bullion about things.'

'Really?' said Betty, who was discovering that she disliked Aubergine Wealth even more than she had thought she did. 'And does he talk back, maybe discuss the price of lettuce?'

'That's enough, little sister,' said Winchflat. 'Everyone's different, you know.'

'Yes, I know,' said Betty. 'There are people who have fun and there are people who don't. And I think it would be fun to take everyone's undies, and fun if we could make lots of money while we did it.'

'I know it's summer, but it still gets quite cool at night,' said Winchflat. 'If we took everyone's underwear now, lot's of them could get chills and the flu.'

'And we could sell them lots of expensive chill

and flu cures,' said Ffiona. 'As well as very expensive knickers.'

Ffiona couldn't believe she had said the word 'knickers' in front of everyone. It was actually quite exciting so she said it again.

'Very expensive knickers,' she continued. 'I mean, everyone wears knickers.'

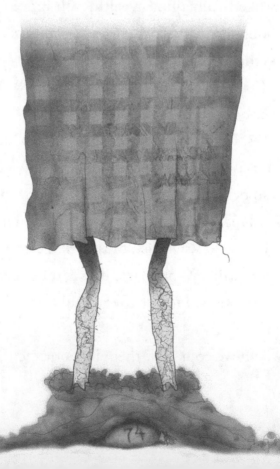

'Apart from Scotsmen and forgetful old ladies,' said Merlinmary.[32]

It was put to the vote and agreed that it would be fun to do. As it had been Betty's idea in the first place, she and Ffiona were put in charge of the operation while everyone else got on with other projects.

Winchflat converted his paper-stealing machine into an Underwear Magnet and showed Betty how to work the controls.

'OK,' he said. 'It's ready to go. You're sure you can remember what to do?'

'Yes,' said Betty. 'The red button's for, er, umm, and the blue one does, er. Yes, it's fine. No problem.'

When everyone had left Betty turned on the machine and the two girls waited while it warmed up. Then Betty pressed the red button except in the

---

[32] *Scotsmen are supposed to wear nothing underneath their kilts. This, of course, is to scare their enemies and is probably a complete lie. After all, it is very cold in Scotland. So if you ever meet a Scotsman wearing a skirt and he has got a very high voice, then he is probably not so much a Scotsman as a Scotswoman. Probably the safest thing to do is play it safe and go and live in Belgium, where the men wear trousers.*

split second before she pressed it, she realised there were three red buttons and it might have been the blue button she was supposed to press, but it was too late to stop.

'Or maybe it was the green one,' she said.

Suddenly the air was filled with knickers of all shapes and sizes and colours. Once again, they travelled through solid walls and out into the street, where they made a beautiful sight, like multi-coloured confetti. Once again, they floated out to sea and formed into large clouds before suddenly vanishing. But instead of re-materialising in great piles in the Caves of Huge Darkness, they turned round and flew back towards New York.

This took about fifteen minutes, more than enough time for everyone to realise their knickers had vanished and begin freaking out. And of course it hadn't just been the ones they were wearing, but all the other pairs they had in drawers, laundry baskets and washing machines, not to mention all the new pairs in shops everywhere. They had all vanished.

And then as suddenly as all the undies had

vanished, they re-appeared. Except not in the same places. Very large people now found themselves squeezed too tightly into tiny little bikini bottoms and the only way to get them off was by cutting them up with scissors. Very thin people found themselves in huge baggy bloomers that fell down to their ankles as soon as they stood up. Men discovered their snug cool white undies were now bright pink with lace trimmings. Not one single garment went back to where it had come from, and although there were some strange people who liked what they were suddenly wearing, most people were too embarrassed to talk about it or even leave the house.

It was then that Ffiona pointed out that, although the whole thing had been a lot of fun, they hadn't actually made a single cent out of it.

'You should have pressed the blue button, little sister,' said Winchflat when the girls took him aside and told him what had happened. 'The Headmaster and Mr Wealth are going to be a bit cross. They've gone and bought millions of shares in underwear factories.'

'Ahh, yes. Hadn't thought of that,' said Betty.

'Maybe we could change all the underwear into something else?' Ffiona suggested.

'Tricky, but it is possible,' said Winchflat. 'I'll have to make some modifications to the Underwear Magnet.'

'Brilliant,' said Betty. 'You are, like, the best big brother in the world.'

'Yes, and you will owe me big time,' said Winchflat. 'So what shall we change everyone's undies into? Bear in mind we don't want to choose anything that might kill or maim people.'

'How about pasta?' said Ffiona. 'That wouldn't hurt anyone. It would be very sticky and unpleasant, but it would actually hurt anyone.'

'It might if they had coeliac disease and couldn't eat wheat,' said Winchflat.

'Could you make it, like, soya bean pasta?' said Betty.

'That wouldn't work either,' said Ffiona. 'All the hippies would love that.'

'Actually, I think we'll be all right with regular

pasta,' said Winchflat. 'I don't think the coeliacs would get sick unless they ate their undies and anyone who eats knickers deserves all they get.'

'OK. I like the pasta,' said Betty, 'but could we change the undies into something else?'

'Why?'

'It'd be funnier,' said Betty.

'Like what?'

'How about cardigans?' said Betty. 'Everyone

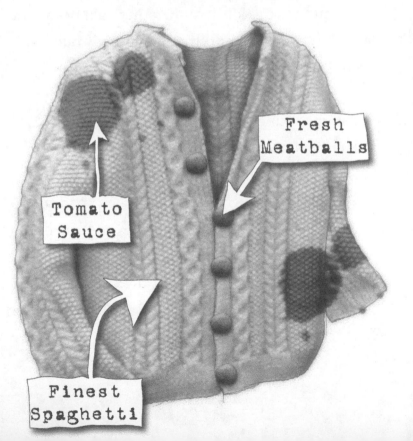

Fresh Meatballs

Tomato Sauce

Finest Spaghetti

with any taste knows that cardigans are evil. That's why they are banned in Transylvania Waters.'

'All right,' said Winchflat, shaking his head and grinning, which scared the life out of a small mouse sitting up in the rafters. 'That's what it'll be, cardigans knitted out of spaghetti.'

'With some yukky used tissues in one pocket,' said Ffiona.

'OK,' said Winchflat.

'And a live goldfish in the other,' said Betty, but Winchflat refused to do that because it would have been cruel.

'Well, I must say I absolutely agree with you about the evilness of cardigans,' said Ffiona. 'And I shall be forever grateful that your family got my parents out of them.'

'Yes, it was touch and go with them for a while,' said Betty. 'But look how well they've turned out now. Why, you're almost like wizards.'

Ffiona thought that was the nicest thing anyone had ever said to her and, with tears in her eyes, gave Betty a big hug.

80

The next morning, the streets were almost deserted. Unlike the toilet-roll shortage, when people scoured the city looking for paper, most people were too embarrassed or uncomfortable to go out. In fact, at seven-thirty that morning, seventy-six-point-three per cent of the population were standing in their showers trying to wash the sticky pasta off their bodies and discovering that spaghetti has a strange knack of wriggling its way into all sorts of nooks and crannies anywhere it can on the human body. There were tears before breakfast and over seven thousand billion swearwords shouted in very loud voices.

The telephone lines, on the other hand, were so

congested with people trying to buy knickers that the whole system crashed. This had a catastrophic effect on the Stock Exchange, where most of the business involved using telephones and faxes. The few screens that were working showed share prices plummeting, so for Aubergine Wealth and Winchflat it was not so much catastrophic as totally brilliant. They bought everything they could lay their hands on for pennies and by lunchtime the pennies had grown into dollars and by the end of the day, the dollars had grown into Huge Piles of Millions of Money. They did particularly well with shares in companies that made products for cleaning drains blocked up with soggy pasta.

All the people who had lost the millions were forced to sell everything they had and it seemed the only one who had any money to buy their stuff was a very small company which, until then, no one had heard of. Le Inondazioni[33] Olive Oil Import and Export Company was located in a very small

---

[33] *By the way, Inondazioni is Italian for Floods.*

shop in a poor part of New York. None of their neighbours knew anything about them, which was hardly surprising as they hadn't been there the day before. At the same time Winchflat had created the very small shop by shuffling all the other buildings in the street up a little bit to create a space for it, he had also implanted false memories in everyone's brains that told them the shop had been there as long as they could remember and the brothers who ran the business – Morboso e Silenzioso Inondazione – were two of the nicest young men you could ever meet. They helped old ladies across the street and fed sardines to abandoned kittens.

'Or maybe,' said a neighbour who hadn't quite caught the full force of Winchflat's Memory-Implanting-Machine, 'they helped kittens across the street and fed sardines to abandoned old ladies.'

By the end of the week, Le Inondazioni Olive Oil Import and Export Company owned more property in New York than anyone else. Just to show what lovely caring people the owners were, they began giving away free knickers to anyone who

asked for them – which, in a city of nineteen million people, was a lot of underwear.

'It is my belief,' said a local councillor, 'that one of the Inondazione brothers should run for Mayor of our great city.'

'Absolutely,' said hundreds of other people, 'and the other one should be Deputy Mayor.'

By an amazing coincidence – which Winchflat created with his newest and probably greatest invention, The Amazing Coincidence Engine[34] – the closing date for nominations to be Mayor was the very next day, with the elections to take place a week later.

'I think if we handle this properly,' said the Headmaster, 'the success of our Summer School could exceed everyone's wildest and most optimistic dreams.'

'Indeed, Headmaster,' said Aubergine Wealth. 'There is an old story that says the original settlers

---

[34] *See the back of the book for more information, including proof that Winchflat may have had other lifetimes before this one, or not.*

84

bought the land New York stands on from the Native Americans for a bag of toffees and some corn or something like that.'

'What flavour?' said Merlinmary.

'What?'

'What flavour were the toffees?'

'I don't know,' said Aubergine. 'That's not the point. The point I'm trying to make is that although everyone thinks it is really funny that they conned the land out of the Native Americans for almost nothing, I think they paid too much. If we handle this correctly, we could end up owning New York without paying a cent for it.'

'So does that mean we get to keep the toffees?' said Merlinmary.

'Forget the toffees,' said Aubergine Wealth.

'That's easy for you to say, but I happen to like toffees,' said Merlinmary.

'Well, listen,' said Winchflat, 'if our plan comes off, you will be able to have all the toffees you could ever want.'

'Could I be the Minister for Toffees?'

'You could indeed.'

'With special powers over treacle toffee?'

'Absolutely.'

'Brilliant,' said Merlinmary.

'Yes, yes, you go off and do that while we take over the city,' said Aubergine Wealth.

'I don't suppose there's going to be a government department for rubber balls, is there?' said Satanella.

With the dream of owning the whole of New York making him feel giddy with desire and happiness, these minor distractions were beginning to make Aubergine Wealth a little short-tempered. Luckily his wizard powers were nowhere nearly as strong as any of the Floods' powers. The most his limited powers could achieve was to turn all the coins in everyone's pockets into chocolate money. Some people thought this was a brilliant talent, but most people got rather annoyed when he did it. He had been able to turn chocolate money into real money, but had that spell removed when several small children nearly choked to death.

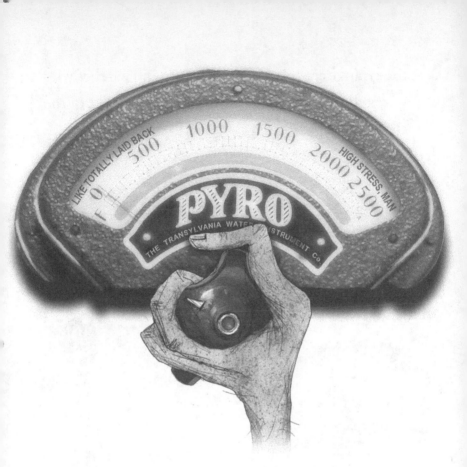

Just to be on the safe side, Winchflat had engaged the I'm-Slightly-Stressed-But-Not-Enough-To-Hurt-Anyone-Drive on his Memory-Implanting-Machine. This was a safety feature he had incorporated in case anyone got annoyed when they discovered that the big expensive property they had paid a fortune for a few years earlier now belonged to a strange crowd of junior wizards and witches who were telling them they either had to move out of the city or start paying rent.

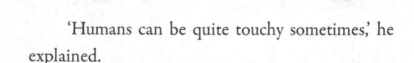

'Humans can be quite touchy sometimes,' he explained.

A week later the election drew the highest turnout in any election of any sort in America ever. The night before, thousands of people had gone to

bed thinking, *Vote? I don't think I'll bother. I mean, it won't make any difference who gets in. Everyone knows all politicians are corrupt.*

However, during the night Winchflat put his Wonderful-Memory-Implanting-Machine into turbo mode and the next morning every single person in New York who was old enough to vote woke up thinking, *Wow, I wonder what time the voting stations open. I can't wait to go and vote for those wonderful Inondazione brothers. They really seem the type of guys to get the city moving again. I mean, how could you not love and trust people who help stray kittens across the street and feed old ladies sardines?*

People who thought in many different languages, people who had never had a single thought before, and even the other election candidates all had the same idea etched into their brains. Winchflat's wonderful machine, which shall be forever known as Winchflat's Wonderful Machine, had worked its magic on everyone. So that when Morbid and Silent got one hundred per cent of the vote with not one single vote going to any of the eighty-seven other candidates, no one was at all suspicious. Far from it, they were delighted.

So Morbid Flood became the Mayor of New York and Silent the Deputy Mayor. The first thing they did was make every single Monday a public holiday. When, a week later, they made every Saturday a working day so the weekends were still only two days long, no one seemed to notice.

'There is no doubt,' said Morbid, 'it's exactly as the famous old wizard philosopher Aristhrottle said all those centuries ago: "Humans are stupid."'

'Indeed,' said Silent. 'In fact, they are so thick that not one of them batted an eyelid when Satanella set up the Department of Rubber Balls.'[35] [36]

---

[35] *The purpose of the Department of Rubber Balls was to charge everyone who had a rubber ball that wasn't red a tax of two dollars a week because of the unnecessary suffering it caused to dogs. In six weeks the tax raised $114,000, but as everyone gradually changed over to exclusively red-coloured balls the income dwindled until the only people paying the tax were colour-blind.*

[36] *My editor has told me that dogs are red-green colourblind. Now, I know I am and so is my daughter Hannah, but I am going to pretend dogs are not. Anyway, it doesn't matter because*

'And no one complained about the Department of Toffees,' said Merlinmary. 'The Toffee Police have been collecting thousands of them.'

Of course, it wasn't just Winchflat's amazing memory machine that made them win. It was also the fact that every pair of free knickers the twins had handed out were printed with Inondazioni For Mayor in bright yellow letters all over them.

Not all of the money that went into the Floods' Enormous Treasure Chests was just to make them the richest wizards in the whole history of history. Greed on that scale would have been despicable. No, the Mayor and his government officers made sure that everyone knew that part of their taxes was being given to those less fortunate than themselves.

An emergency charity was set up to deliver red rubber balls to all the dogs in New York City. As the new Mayor said in a television interview, 'No dog shall go to bed cold or hungry or without a red rubber ball to call its own.' Because of Winchflat's

ALL dogs know that Red Rubber Balls give off a magical aura that no other coloured ball does.

Wonderful Machine, the entire population of New York totally loved dogs and were only too happy to know their money had helped fix a serious Red-Rubber-Ball-Shortage situation.

This meant that all the cats in New York were forced to move to another country. When the draw was held to decide which country all the cats should go to, Satanella picked the winning country and incredibly, it was Belgium.[37] The next morning Belgians woke up to find thousands of New York cats inside their houses meowing in American, which of course none of them could understand.[38]

---

[37] *Actually it wasn't incredible because every one of the three-hundred-and-fifteen pieces of paper in the lottery hat had 'Belgium' written on them, and of course, sending all of the city's cats to Belgium was a win-win situation for everyone except the cats, cat lovers and Belgium, but that's OK because they don't count. Small defenceless birds everywhere were delighted.*

[38] *This was probably a good thing because apart from 'Where's my breakfast?', the rest of the meowing involved a lot of very strong swearwords.*

Generally, good things are usually too good to last and so it was in New York. It went something like this...

'OK,' said Aubergine Wealth when the students were all gathered for the evening conference. 'We pretty well own everything that's worth owning in New York and it's been ridiculously easy. In fact, it's been not that great a challenge at all, really. So has anyone got any suggestions about what we could do next?'

'Well, we've actually only got two weeks until the end of the summer holidays,' said the Headmaster. 'So we need to wrap things up here so we can all have a week's rest before next term back at Quicklime's.'

'What do you mean, wrap things up?' said Morbid.

'Put everything back how it was before Summer School started,' said the Headmaster. 'This was only ever meant to be a project, something for you all to learn a bit about how the financial world worked.'

'But Headmaster . . .' Aubergine Wealth began, turning a terrible shade of white. 'Please, Headmaster, tell me that what I'm thinking isn't true?'

'That depends on what you are thinking.'

'Well, Headmaster,' Aubergine Wealth said as he felt all the blood drain away from the pocket where he kept his wallet full of platinum credit cards, 'it sounds like you want us to give everything back.'

'Well, yes, of course,' said the Headmaster. 'I thought everyone realised that.'

They didn't.

Some of the teachers and students were more upset than others.

'But, but,' said Morbid, 'in case you'd forgotten,

I'm actually the Mayor of New York. So what are we supposed to do about that?'

'Oh come on,' said the Headmaster. 'You didn't really think a twelve-year-old wizard could be in charge of all this, did you?'

'But everyone voted for me,' said Morbid. 'Everyone.'

'Well, no, what actually happened was that Winchflat used his Wonderful-Memory-Implanting-Machine to persuade everyone to vote for you,' said the Headmaster.

'Well, yes, but they did vote.'

'And now they are all going to unvote,' said the Headmaster. 'Tomorrow morning when they wake up, everyone will have totally forgotten about that election and they'll all be looking forward to voting next week, and you will not be one of the candidates because you will be back at Quicklime's learning your eighty-five-and-a-quarter times table with everyone else.'

'And what about all the money and the lovely penthouses and all the other stuff?' said Merlinmary.

'Can't we keep any of it?'

'No, it all has to go back to its rightful owners.'

'That's us, isn't it?' said Satanella. 'We didn't break any laws to get it all. So we should be allowed to keep it.'

'I think using powerful spells and crafty wizardry might not strictly be against the law,' said the Headmaster, 'but it's probably pretty close.'

'Excuse me, Headmaster,' Aubergine Wealth whimpered, 'but isn't that what being a wizard is all about? Isn't magic our reward for being persecuted by human beings who are, after all, considerably more stupid than even the most stupid wizard who ever lived?'[39]

'Well, yes, but the first law of wizardry is that we must not harm humans,' said the Headmaster.

---

[39] *The most stupid wizard who has ever lived is Floella Yardstyck, who lives in a small valley on the far side of Lake Tarnish. She is Transylvania Waters's only person who is known as a Living Legend, which is a term humans use for very stupid people who can stand up and speak their name at the same time. If they play sport or sing really badly then they are called a Super Living Legend.*

'No it isn't,' said Aubergine Wealth. 'That's the first law of robotics.'

'Really?'

'Yes,' said Aubergine Wealth.

'Oh.'

'So does that mean we can keep all the stuff?'

'No it does not,' said the Headmaster. 'And be aware, all of you, that you are under the Painful Pimples Spell, which means that if you keep anything at all, you will get great big yellow spots that will be very painful and burst at extremely embarrassing times. One pimple for each thing you keep.'

There was panic followed by a lot of clattering as everyone emptied their pockets. Rolls of dollar bills, exquisite jewellery, gold watches and a strange assortment of small electronic gadgets covered the floor. Dozens of pieces of paper, title deeds to fabulous apartments and stocks and shares fluttered everywhere.

The Headmaster reached into his gown and pulled out the Quicklime College Supreme Wand. He threw it into the air and it flew around the room

just above everyone's heads before returning to his hand. There was a brilliant white flash of light and all the treasure vanished, transported back to its original owners. At the same time a lovely peaceful calm descended on everyone so they didn't actually mind losing all their treasures. And, to top it off, everyone got a special Show Bag with lots of sugar-filled lollies, a chocolate broomstick and a free pair of Mordonna Flood sunglasses.

The Headmaster had anticipated there might be a few objections to putting everything back and he had made sure he was prepared. Not only had he brought the wand – the first time in living memory it had ever been outside the remote valley in Patagonia where Quicklime College was situated – but Winchflat's Wonderful-Memory-Implanting-Machine had actually been the Headmaster's idea.

It never occurred to any of the students that the machine could work on them. They were, after all, witches and wizards, which meant their brains were several thousand times more advanced than human brains. So everyone assumed that they would be immune to memory implanting. The only two people who knew this wasn't the case were Winchflat and the Headmaster. It had been one of the main things they had talked about when they had discussed the possibility of building a Wonderful-Memory-Implanting-Machine in the first place.

'You know what people, even witches and wizards, can be like when large amounts of money are involved,' the Headmaster had said. 'If you could create this machine, it would give us some insurance in the event of any arguments at the end of the holidays.'

Winchflat agreed and that was how the machine came to be built.

'Of course, no one must ever know that we discussed this,' said the Headmaster. 'And if it ever comes out, I will deny any involvement.'

'If it ever comes out, Headmaster,' said Winchflat, 'I can soon fix it with a quick memory implant. See, it has its own insurance built in.'

'Brilliant,' said the Headmaster, wishing that every Quicklime's student could be a genius like his star pupil.

Though if they actually were, he thought, *I would be out of a job.*

Winchflat sat quietly in the shadows at the back of the room, twiddling the knobs on the Wonderful-Memory-Implanting-Machine, and one by one everyone agreed that the Headmaster was right. Everything had to be put back exactly as it had been, not just the stuff that had just been sent back, but all the strange events that had happened since the Summer School had begun.

Well, not so much put back absolutely, totally, exactly as it had been, but in many cases a bit better. The toilet rolls were softer. The sun shone a bit more each day, but it didn't get so unbearably hot and dusty. The birds all sang a bit sweeter and the cats that had been brought back from Belgium were now cross-eyed so they couldn't catch the birds.

It didn't take much magic to make the mayoral elections that Morbid had won the week before never have happened. Now they were due next week. Although the candidate who would be the winner was actually quite a decent person, there's always room for improvement. So Winchflat improved him and within one month of being elected, he had got rid of three thousand, eight hundred and seventy-five stupid, petty little laws that only made people's lives more restricted and miserable, though it was still illegal to fart in front of a nun on Sundays.[40]

BUT not everyone was happy. Standing in the shadows, almost hidden behind the blood-red velvet curtains, out of range of the Painful Pimples Spell and protected from the Wonderful-Memory-Implanting-Machine by a layer of lead implanted under his scalp, there was one person who was most definitely not at all happy.

Aubergine Wealth.

At the first talk of giving everything back, he had come over all faint and had to go outside for some fresh air. When his head had cleared he slipped back into the room and stood silently in the darkest corner, his head whirling with confusion and

---

[40] *Actually, he didn't so much abolish them as give them away to England, helping to make Britain one of the most controlled nanny states in the so-called free world.*

desperate plans. Parting with five cents gave him a headache. Giving up a dollar gave him a headache and a nose-bleed. And losing fifty dollars gave him a migraine and nose-and-ear-bleed and severe conniptions.[41] The thought of having to give back the millions of dollars, portfolio of stock and shares and collection of wonderful penthouse apartments he had acquired over the previous weeks was more than he could stand. There was no way that was going to happen. If it meant leaving his beloved Quicklime College, then that was a price he was prepared to pay, although even the words 'price he was prepared to pay' were very upsetting.

He felt his whole being about to explode in uncontrolled rage. Yet he managed to stand completely still and silent. This he only managed to do by swallowing his own tongue. He stopped the

---

[41] *Conniption is such a brilliant word, I am quite upset to realise that it has taken until* The Floods Book 9 *to use it. I will try harder and make sure I have conniptions in every other Floods book from now on. Conniptions are particularly nice on sourdough toast with finely chopped lettuce and mint sauce. No, that's not right. That's bacon.*

steam inside his head from bursting out by biting off his little fingers and stuffing one in each ear. He grew faint from loss of blood, yet these sacrifices were worth the prizes the Summer School had brought him. He slid down behind the heavy curtains and fell into unconsciousness. No one noticed even when a thin trickle of blood crawled out from beneath the curtains and vanished into a crack in the floorboards.

Damn, curses and damn, he thought at the thought of parting with some of his precious blood.

8

'**I** think we should have a souvenir of our time here,' said the Headmaster. 'Something big that says NEW YORK.'

'Well, there's plenty of big stuff in America,' said Betty. 'They're always going on about how everything they've got is bigger than everyone else's.'

'Their bottoms are,' said Ffiona.

'And their food,' said the Cook.

'I think I have the perfect suggestion,' said Winchflat, 'but we'll do it in the middle of the night when everyone is asleep.'

'There is never a time when everyone's asleep,'

said Betty. 'After all, New York is called The City That Never Sleeps.'

'I thought that was Antwerp,' said Ffiona, who was a bit of a geography nerd.

'No, no,' said the Headmaster. 'I think you'll find that Antwerp is The City That Sleeps In Late Every Morning.'

'I thought that was Buenos Aires,' said Merlinmary.

'No, that's The City That Sleeps Every Afternoon,' said Winchflat, turning on his Wonderful-Memory-Implanting-Machine. 'Anyway, a few quick adjustments and tonight New York will be The City That Decided To Have An Early Night.'

So they packed their bags and removed every tiny scrap of evidence that might show any of them had been in New York. Then they transferred ownership of the Summer School building to a charity for sad, lost, lonely puppies. They removed all evidence of Le Inondazioni Olive Oil Import and Export Company and shuffled the buildings back to fill the gap they had created for it. Winchflat did the best he could with his Wonderful Machine to erase all memories of the election and Morbid becoming Mayor and the Great No Toilet Roll Pandemic, but for weeks afterwards every New Yorker was left with a head full of the uneasy feeling that something wasn't quite right though they could never put their finger on it.[42] The huge numbers of red rubber balls everywhere only added to the confusion.

But all of that was nothing compared to the thing the Floods took away with them when they left.

'And you must admit,' said Winchflat as he stood on the steps of Castle Twilight back in Transylvania Waters, looking out over the town towards Lake Tarnish where it now stood, 'the Statue of Liberty looks a lot better here than it did in America.'

'Indeed it does, darling,' said Mordonna. 'And the wizard's hat is a great improvement.'

---

[42] *I think you'll actually find that this is how New Yorkers always feel.*

9

The next week was spent catching up with the laundry, sleeping a lot and generally doing nothing before it was time for school to start again. Everyone was so busy that no one actually noticed Aubergine Wealth was not around. Even though he had been born there, he didn't live in Transylvania Waters so no one realised he hadn't gone home. He had a house in Switzerland that no one was ever invited to visit and that was where he always spent the holidays. Though he didn't like to think he so much 'spent' the holidays as 'saved' the holidays.

His house was halfway up a mountain overlooking Geneva, and in particular overlooking the six Swiss banks where he had large amounts of his money hidden.

Other places he had his money hidden included:

- *In three hundred cardboard boxes under his bed.*
- *In an enormous sock inside a plastic bag under a rock on Inaccessible Island, guarded by a flock of really bad-tempered Rockhopper Penguins who spent all day hopping on and off the rock and spitting at anyone who ever went near it – which no one did, so wasting all their spit made them even more bad-tempered.*
- *Inside a big tin embedded in a massive block of concrete in the heart of the radioactive Chernobyl nuclear power station.*
- *In a wallet that was so big it took ten men to lift it, except there was no way Aubergine Wealth was going to tell one other person, never mind ten, that he had a huge wallet of cash, so it was slowly sinking into the lawn behind his house, which was as far as he had managed to drag it.*

- *Stuck over every single square metre of every wall in his house, then painted over with pretty flowers to disguise it as wallpaper.*
- *Lots of other places.*
- *Lots more other places.*[43]

When Aubergine Wealth regained consciousness, the Summer School was deserted apart from a large number of sad, lost, lonely puppies who were licking his face very enthusiastically because they were not lost or lonely any more.

There was also another person there, and this person had pulled Aubergine's fingers out of his ears and was sewing them back onto his hands.

The pain was excruciating.

'I expect you are in excruciating pain,' said the lady. 'Don't worry, I can fix that.'

She hit him on the head with a heavy saucepan and instantly all the pain went away, due to a

---

[43] *He also kept several gold coins up each nostril and wore origami underpants folded out of a one-million-dollar bank note.*

sudden outbreak of unconsciousness.

When Aubergine came round, he was lying on a large couch with his head in the lady's lap. She had finished sewing his fingers back on and was bathing his face and hands with a soft warm cloth to remove all the remaining dried blood and puppy drool.

'Tell me, you poor man,' she said. 'Who chopped your fingers off?'

'Well, it's a long story,' Aubergine began.

'I'm in no hurry,' said the lady, stroking his head. 'By the way, I am Chrysanthemum Gofaintly and this is the Manhattan Home For Sad, Lost, Lonely Puppies. The puppies and I are wondering who you are and what you are doing here.'

Aubergine Wealth sat up and looked around. Every last speck of evidence that Quicklime College had ever been there had vanished, even down to the teethmarks Satanella had left in the doorframe and the unmentionable stains on the wallpaper.

'Actually, it's a very long story,' he said. 'And I think you probably wouldn't believe any of it anyway.'

'Sweetheart,' said Chrysanthemum, 'my name is Chrysanthemum. My parents were two wild hippies in California in the nineteen-sixties. I live with two-hundred-and-whatever puppies. I'll believe anything.'

'Do you believe in wizards?'

'Well, of course I do,' said Chrysanthemum. 'Half the people in the commune I grew up in were witches and wizards.'

'No, no. I don't mean long-haired hippies who took strange potions and thought having a bath was a capitalist plot,' said Aubergine Wealth. 'I mean real wizards who can do magic.'

'Hey, baby, everything was magic in the sixties.'

'I mean real magic, like this,' said Aubergine.

He looked around the room and focused on an old armchair covered in sleeping puppies. As he concentrated the chair lifted itself up in the air and floated slowly towards them.

'Oh, that sort of magic,' said Chrysanthemum and fainted.

When she woke up she was lying on her back on the sofa with her head in Aubergine Wealth's lap. The armchair with the sleeping puppies was still floating around the room in lazy circles and now Chrysanthemum and Aubergine's sofa began to float after it.

'Wow,' said Chrysanthemum.

It is an unwritten law that wizards tell humans as little as possible about their world. Very few humans know there is such a country as Transylvania Waters and even fewer know about Quicklime College. For most humans the world of witches and wizards is like it is in story books, all made up and rather silly. True wizards are only too happy to keep it that way. It makes life a lot less complicated.

Since Nerlin had become King of Transylvania Waters and human tourists had begun visiting, things hadn't really changed that much. None of the visitors realised the entire population were wizards. They just thought they were a bit strange, which is what everyone thinks about anyone who comes from a different country to them.

He wasn't sure why, but Aubergine felt completely overwhelmed with a great need to tell Chrysanthemum Gofaintly everything.

Chrysanthemum was a sweet, floaty hippy who thought everything in the world could be put right with a nice vase of flowers and some homeopathic

ylang-ylang drops. Aubergine Wealth was a hard-nosed, soulless businessman who thought everything in the world could be put right by everyone giving him all their money.

Well, my world would be put right, he thought. *Who cares about anyone else's?*

Yet he felt deeply attracted to Chrysanthemum. Sure, she was the only person who had ever sewn his fingers back on, but there was more to it than that. Whatever it was didn't fit in with anything he had learned up until that point. It had nothing to do with spreadsheets and calculators or the rise and fall of the value of gold, so he was confused. For the first time in his life the faintest hint of the tiniest possibility that there might be more to life than money crept into the edge of his brain.

Don't be ridiculous, his brain said, but his heart said, *Hey, man, think about it.*

Chrysanthemum Gofaintly also felt deeply attracted to Aubergine. Sure, he was the first man she had ever sewn bits of his body back onto and he was the first man she had ever felt sweet thoughts for who didn't need a haircut and a wash, but there was more to it than that.

He had a strange hypnotic smell and she sensed that beneath his apparently soulless exterior there was the heart of a true romantic. She could see the two of them growing broccoli and radishes together in a little cottage by a beautiful lake while a large number of once sad, lost and lonely puppies scampered playfully in the soft grass biting the heads off tiny lizards. That last bit confused her a little, but she let it pass and concentrated on the organic vegetables.

So Aubergine Wealth sat the lovely Chrysanthemum Gofaintly on his knee and told her everything. He told her not just about teaching at Quicklime College and the Summer School, but everything right back to his earliest memory, which was selling his Lego for eighty-five per cent profit to another child at pre-school. He told her that by recycling his disposable nappies and selling his baby teeth on eBay he had become a millionaire at the age of five and that by the time he was ten he had been a billionaire.

Chrysanthemum Gofaintly was enchanted. Did she think to herself, here was a man who she could save from the mercenary grip of capitalism and lead down the path of inner peace, yoga and Buddhist contentment into a world of the simple country life and living happily ever after? Did she see her future making this lost, wealth-obsessed man realise his full potential in a higher level of meditation, cuddly puppies and organic vegies?

No, she didn't.

She suddenly realised that she had needs too. Big, unfulfilled needs she had kept locked away in her heart for years.

Stuff the broccoli and radishes, she thought. *Stuff the poor defenceless animals. SHOW ME THE MONEY!*

And then she realised what the strange, hypnotic smell was. It was a heady, delirious smell that made a vase of roses smell like nothing more than a bunch of flowers. It was the scent of money, rolls of hundred-dollar notes bursting from Aubergine's every pocket. To the child of penniless hippies all this was a whole new world. The most money Chrysanthemum had ever had in her hands in one go was twelve dollars and she had thought the fact she could buy three chickpea burgers and a litre of wheatgrass all at once had been pretty cool.

Now as Aubergine rose to his feet, he just leaked money everywhere. Notes fluttered around like very big butterflies, only much more beautiful. Chrysanthemum picked them out of the air and buried her face in them. She breathed in the scent of wealth, closed her eyes and sighed as a gentle smile of paradise spread across her face.

Stuff meditation. Stuff Zen Buddhism, she thought. *This is pure nirvana.*

And you are the most perfect woman in the world, thought Aubergine, who knew the look of money-worship when he saw it.

'All those years I wasted,' said Chrysanthemum. 'All that floaty hippy rubbish, living on tofu and tinkly bells and dopey chanting. When all the time paradise was right here.'

Aubergine thought he had died and gone to

heaven. All those years he had spent collecting more and more wealth without stopping for a second to ask himself why. Now he knew. Now he had someone to lavish all his incredibly massive amounts of money on.

'I don't suppose,' he said nervously. 'I don't suppose you would consider marrying me, would you?'

'I would,' said Chrysanthemum. 'Have you got all the paperwork?'

'Paperwork?'

'Yes, the pre-nuptial agreements and contracts.'

'Do we need all that?' said Aubergine.

'I just assumed . . .' Chrysanthemum began.

'Do you think Romeo and Juliet had paperwork?'

'Well, no, but then look what happened to them,' said Chrysanthemum.

'No, what I meant was it doesn't seem very romantic.'

Chrysanthemum knew that Aubergine Wealth loved her more than she could have ever imagined. For someone so staggeringly wealthy to marry someone with no contracts to protect them, they would have to be really, really in love, or stupid, and Chrysanthemum knew that Aubergine was definitely not stupid.

'Wow,' she whispered.

'Of course, there could be a few problems,' said Aubergine Wealth.

'Well, of course there could. It's only to be expected,' said Chrysanthemum. 'Two people who have been single for years, suddenly being married. It's going to take a bit of getting used to for both of us.'

'No, my beloved, that wasn't what I meant,' said Aubergine. 'I meant that Quicklime College will probably be looking for me. I have seventeen billion dollars or so that they want me to give back to the people I acquired it from.'

'That's ridiculous,' said Chrysanthemum Gofaintly. 'Did you break the law to get any of it?'

'Not quite.'

'Well then, it's yours to keep and I'm sure any court in the land would support you.'

'But Quicklime College includes a lot of the most powerful witches and wizards on Earth,' said Aubergine. 'They are more powerful than any court and as far as they are concerned, their rules and laws are above any human laws.'

'Mmm, I see. Well, we'll have to work out a plan,' said Chrysanthemum, 'a plan that does not include giving-it-back options. That is not going to happen.'

Aubergine Wealth knew he had found Miss

Right, Ms Right, Mrs Right and Miss Totally Perfect. There had been a nagging thought in the back of his brain that if all else failed, he could always save himself by doing as he had been ordered. It had made him feel better knowing that he had a potential solution if he really needed it, but the thought of losing it all had also given him an upset stomach and a bad headache.

Now his thoughts were all over the place.[44] He knew what the Floods were capable of. He had heard of their kinder punishments, such as turning children into refrigerators or feeding them to the partly – but not completely – dead Queen Mother. He had also heard rumours of the punishments no one was supposed to know about, such as turning people into Belgian history teachers and, if that worked, turning them inside-out too. There was even the legendary punishment where they had turned a very evil slum-landlord into a frog in the kitchen of

---

[44] *Because they were all inside his head, they were not so much all over the place as racing round, tripping over each other and making him dizzy.*

a French restaurant – not just any frog, but one with ninety big, fat, succulent legs. The list of extremely creative punishments the Floods were rumoured to have meted out to bad people was endless and grew even longer than endless every day. He knew that all the really bad ones were only rumours, but imagination is a powerful weapon, especially when you are the potential victim.

On the other hand, he was now suddenly and totally in love so deeply that he thought he might be possibly, perhaps, maybe prepared to give every last cent of his fortune away if he had to. Giving back the rewards he had earned from the Summer School would be small change compared to the rewards of winning Chrysanthemum's heart.

Well, maybe not all of it, but so much that he would be left with no more than ten or twenty – well, say thirty billion dollars, he thought.

I can't believe I have these thoughts inside my head, he added, *and that I'm even considering them as possibilities.*

But he needn't have worried. As these new

thoughts shocked his brain, Chrysanthemum's brain had also changed dramatically. Step aside, Miss Nice Girl, feeding sardines to little old ladies and helping kittens across the road – Ms Super-Computer-I-Love-Money-Oh-How-I-Love-Money is here. If the little old ladies want sardines, fine, but each one will cost ten dollars, and the kittens will never see the other side of the road. They will see the big fat steamrollers turning them into lovely designer mats to sell in the most exclusive over-priced boutiques. *Mmm, that gives me an idea*, she thought, looking around the room at all the lovely, happy, cuddly puppies.

Thankfully, there was still enough of the old hippy Chrysanthemum left to scratch the kitty carpets and puppy pillows idea.

Phew, she thought. *Money does strange things to a person. A bit like seven very strong espressos, only stronger.*

'So the first thing we must do is find somewhere safe to hide out while we work out the best way to handle all this,' she said.

'No,' said Aubergine Wealth. 'That is the second

thing. The first thing we must do is get married.'

'And we need to do something with all these puppies,' said Chrysanthemum. 'I think travelling

with a hundred and twenty-three very excited incontinent baby dogs might draw a bit of attention to us. Could you do a spell and turn them into skylarks? We could just open the window then and they could all fly away to Central Park. Can wizards do that sort of thing?'

'There are different levels of magic,' said Aubergine. 'To change something that's alive into another life form you need to have the top level – Very Advanced Magic. Unfortunately I've only got Middle Level Magic. I can only do magic on inanimate objects and stuff like that.'

'How do you get Very Advanced Magic? Can you buy it?'

'No. It's mainly hereditary. If your parents had it, then you have it when you're born. The Floods are all like that,' said Aubergine.[45] 'The only other way is for a Grand Master Wizard to give you an upgrade and, as far as I know, there is only one Grand Master Wizard and no one actually knows where he lives. In fact, most people think he's simply a myth.'

'Do you?'

'Yes, but I also think he's real, a kind of living myth,' said Aubergine.[46]

---

[45] *Apart from Betty, who has a strange version of Very Advanced Magic called Unfortunate Magic, where she can theoretically do very advanced magic, but it often comes out wrong.*

[46] *This was completely accurate.*

'If we could find him,' said Chrysanthemum, 'could you bribe him or something like that?'

'The puppies would probably have died of old age before we discovered his secret home and I think anyone who tried to bribe him would end up turned into a small omelette. No, we have to think of something else.'

'OK. Here's my suggestion,' said Chrysanthemum. 'Everyone loves puppies, but not everyone is prepared to give one a home. However, everyone also loves money and everyone loves chocolate. So if we get big bars of chocolate, wrap them in dollar bills and give them away to anyone who is prepared to take a puppy at the same time, we shouldn't have any problem re-homing them.'

Although the thought of giving anything away went against everything Aubergine Wealth believed in, he knew that sometimes you actually had to make small investments to get a bigger return. One hundred and twenty-three bars of chocolate he could produce. His magic was powerful enough for that. Then he scooped up one hundred and twenty-three ten-dollar bills and they wrapped each bar of chocolate in one.

They stood outside the building with a big sign that said:

AMAZING OFFER!!!
FREE chocolate, FREE money
AND A FREE
bonus lovely cuddly puppy!

When humans see the word 'free' the small sensible bit of their brain switches off. In less than fifteen minutes Aubergine and Chrysanthemum were completely puppy-free. They collected up the rest of the money that had been floating round the room and went down to City Hall to get a marriage licence.

'You have to wait for at least twenty-four hours before you can get hitched,' said the clerk.

'Unless there are special circumstances – then we could marry you straight away. Are there any special circumstances?'

Aubergine leant over, whispered in the clerk's ear and handed him an envelope.

'I now pronounce you man and wife,' said the clerk with a big smile. 'You may now kiss the bribe ... oops, sorry. You may now kiss the bride.'

'What did you say?' Chrysanthemum Wealth said as they took a taxi to the airport.

'I asked him if a huge bribe qualified as special circumstances. He said probably. So I gave him the title deeds to the old Summer School puppy shelter apartment block in Manhattan,' said Aubergine.

It wasn't until they reached the airport that they realised they hadn't the faintest idea where they were going. They had been so busy with getting married, it had entirely slipped their minds. They sat down in the cafe and wrote out a list in three columns. The first column was places the school would look first, the second column was places the school would look last and the third column was all the other places the school would look. The third column only had one word in it, but it was the biggest problem.

The word was:

Everywhere.

'So what you're saying is, there's not much point in writing anything in the other two columns, because wherever we go, they will come looking,' said Chrysanthemum.

'Pretty well,' said Aubergine. 'Though I suppose if we could work out the last place they'd look and go there, there's a remote chance they might get bored and stop looking before they get there.'

'Is that likely?'

'Not really, but it's the best chance we've got,' said Aubergine.

'Well, the last place I'd look for someone would be right under my nose behind me,' said Chrysanthemum, 'or Belgium.'

'I think I'd rather get caught than go to Belgium,' said Aubergine. 'Did you know they've got a town called Silly?'

'I did, actually,' said Chrysanthemum. 'When

I was a teenager I spent a summer there working as a nanny to a family of Silly bottle makers. I think I agree with you about going back there.'

'OK, well, that only leaves the option of going right under their noses.'

'What will they do if they catch us?'

'I'm not really sure,' said Aubergine, 'but it won't be nice. You have to remember that the Floods are the most powerful wizards in creation.[47] I mean, they don't just make armchairs of puppies float round the room. They could make the whole apartment block where the room is float around and not just around the street, but off around the moon and back, and when it got back the puppies on the armchair in that room on the fifth floor would have changed into sabre-tooth goldfish that breathe fire and speak Welsh.'

'Really?'

---

[47] *Apart from the Legendary Grand Master Wizard who is so legendary he may not actually exist, or may just be messing with our minds to make us think that he might not exist when he really does, or doesn't. Or both.*

'Oh yes, they've done it before – and that was just because someone gave them fifty cents short in their change when they bought a cabbage. We're running away with billions.'

'So, do you think they're out looking for you now?' said Chrysanthemum.

'Probably not,' said Aubergine. 'I reckon they won't realise I'm missing until school starts next week and I'm not there.'

'How about lying?'

'What do you mean?'

'Why not just go back to school as if nothing has happened and if they say anything, just say you gave everything to the lady who took over the Summer School building for the Manhattan Home For Lost & Lonely Puppies?'

'That's you.'

'Oh yes, so it is,' said Chrysanthemum with a big grin.

This was not a cheating grin that meant she was about to rob Aubergine. It was a conspiratorial, naughty grin that meant they were both about to

con the Floods, which if it worked would be the first time in history, apart from the time Mordonna's father, ex-King Quatorze, took over the whole of Transylvania Waters. Compared to that, keeping a few billion dollars didn't seem so bad.

'The Headmaster tells me that Aubergine Wealth has gone missing,' said Nerlin at dinner that night. 'There's no one at his home in Switzerland, nor has he been anywhere near his secret hideaways that we're not supposed to know about. The Headmaster sent people to check. They say that the Belgian Fish Repair Shop where he has a secret apartment, the Leek Weaving Works in Wales where he has another hidey hole and the Potato Museum on Tristan da Cunha are all deserted. No one has been anywhere near them in months. It would appear that Mr Wealth and the seventeen-billion-plus dollars he made at the Summer School have done a runner.'

The Floods and the Hulberts were all gathered in the Friday Night Dining Room at Castle Twilight to celebrate the fact that it was Friday night and dinner time.

'I suspect that Mr Wealth thinks we don't know what he's done,' Nerlin continued. 'He probably thinks he's safe until school starts next week and we'll all assume he's gone on holiday.'

'Maybe he has,' said Ffiona.

'Mr Wealth does not do holidays,' said Nerlin. 'He thinks they are a waste of money.'

'Don't worry,' said Mordonna, putting her arm round Winchflat's shoulders. 'Once again our resident genius is in control of the situation.'

When Aubergine Wealth had passed out behind the curtain back in Manhattan, he thought no one had realised he was there. When he had come to and everyone else had gone back to Transylvania Waters, he was sure that no one had known he hadn't gone with them. There had been a lot of things going on, what with transferring all the wealth back to its original owners and removing every single trace of the Summer School. So it had been a fair assumption. After all, who would miss one person, especially one person who didn't actually have any friends to look out for him?[48]

But Winchflat had noticed because Winchflat noticed absolutely everything, even the numbers of feathers on the left wing of a sparrow that had been sitting on the windowsill outside the room where they were having their last Summer School meeting.[49] He hadn't been able to count the feathers on the sparrow's right wing as it was sitting sideways. Although he assumed it was the same, he wasn't happy with guessing and decided at some point in the future he would have to make a machine to let

---

[48] *Until he met Chrysanthemum, Aubergine's best friend had been his pocket calculator and even that hadn't liked him very much because Aubergine could do financial calculations a lot faster than it could. Adding two and two, he couldn't do, but adding two billion and four thousand and nine he could do with his eyes shut. In fact, he could even do it with his eyes wide open just as long as the numbers he was adding were money and not vegetables or sheep.*

[49] *Forty-three.*

him see through sparrows so he could count all the feathers with complete accuracy. With such an eye for detail, it would have been surprising if he hadn't seen Aubergine. He had even noted exactly how much blood the economics teacher had lost as it trickled down the crack in the floorboards.[50]

Mmm, clever, he thought when he discovered the anti-spell lead shield buried under Aubergine's scalp, but it only took a couple of seconds to lift a tiny bit of the lead and slip a bugging device into his brain. If Aubergine discovered it, he would assume that the lead was blocking the device's signals, which of course it wasn't. It took more than some heavy metal to outsmart Winchflat.

'So where is he now?' said Nerlin.

'They are at JFK airport,' said Winchflat, 'trying to decide where to fly to.'

'They?' said Mordonna.

'Yes. Aubergine Wealth appears to have got married.'

---

[50] *Twenty-three cubic centimetres.*

136

'Are you sure?' said the Headmaster. 'When you say married, you do mean to another living person and not a pocket calculator or a spreadsheet?'

'No, it's a person,' said Winchflat. 'A human being.'

'Not a witch?'

'No, it's an ordinary human. If it was a witch, my bug would say so.'

'And can your bug tell us what they are saying?' said Nerlin.

'Only what he is saying, not her,' said Winchflat. 'I can usually tailor bugging devices for each situation, but Mr Wealth getting married was not a possibility that I thought was remotely likely.'

Aubergine and Chrysanthemum decided they would go back to Transylvania Waters, and not some remote part as far away from Castle Twilight as possible, but to a small house built right into the outer wall of the castle itself. They also decided that to avoid detection, they would actually fly to Belgium and then travel the rest of the way by horse and cart. Belgium would be the last place the Floods would expect them to go. They bought their plane tickets and went through security and, of course, as soon as Aubergine stepped into the electronic scanner, the lead shield in his head set off all the alarms.

'Take your shoes off, please, sir,' said the security officer.

'Take your belt off, please, sir,' the officer said when that made no difference. 'Pull your trousers up, please, sir.'

This went on until Aubergine Wealth was down to his underpants and small children were hiding in tears behind their parents. Actually everyone was hiding behind something because Aubergine Wealth in his undies was a sight that no living creature should be made to look at. Even Chrysanthemum, who adored her new husband, felt herself beginning to go faint. It wasn't because he was displaying anything rude so much as the strange colour and texture of his skin. It was like pea-soup-coloured corrugated cardboard that had been soaking in water for a very long time.

But even then Aubergine Wealth set off the security alarm each time so they took him away to a special x-ray room and scanned him. As soon as they did that everyone could see his lead anti-spell head shield and that explained everything. Aubergine had been watching the screen too and that was when he saw Winchflat's secret tracking device.

I wondered why I had a bit of a headache when I came to, he thought.

He was just about to tell Chrysanthemum about the bug when he stopped himself. He guessed that Winchflat – and it had to be him because no one else was clever enough – could hear every word he was saying. He motioned to Chrysanthemum to say nothing and scribbled her a note explaining the situation.

Brilliant, Chrysanthemum wrote back. *If we play this right it could work to our advantage.*

What's your plan? wrote Aubergine, quite happy for his wife to take charge.

First we will buy two airplane tickets for Mongolia, she explained. *When we get there, we will remove the bug from your head and implant it into a yak. The Flood boy will track the yak through the wilds of Mongolia while we travel on the Trans-Siberian railway back to eastern Europe where we will slip into Transylvania Waters disguised as tourists.*

Brilliant, Aubergine scribbled, falling in love with Chrysanthemum all over again – which was a bit confusing because he hadn't fallen out of love with her since the first time.

'I think we should go to Mongolia,' Aubergine said in a loud clear voice. 'No one will ever look for us there.'

'They've just bought two tickets for Mongolia,' said Winchflat.

'Are you sure?' said Mordonna. 'It seems a bit of an obvious place to go.'

'That is true,' said Winchflat, 'but I think that's

why they're going there. They'll think it's so obvious that we won't expect them to go there.'

'It's all beyond me,' said Nerlin, but then there were a lot of things that were beyond him. He may have been Top Wizard by the fact of being King of Transylvania Waters, but wizards are like humans in that respect. Hardly anyone is king of anywhere because they are intelligent or resourceful. They usually get the job because their dad had it and he got it from his dad and so on back in history until the first ancestor became king by killing everyone else who wanted the job. The fact that they are not

Unlike other royal families, the Floods did NOT wear dead animals on their hats and necks.

Nerlin is seen here wearing Andrew and Christine – the two Royal Ermine, who are very much alive.

best friends with thinking is probably quite a good thing. Otherwise they would just sit there feeling really guilty at having all that privilege without having earned any of it.[51]

'Mmm, the old double-bluff trick,' said the Headmaster. 'It's that sort of devious thinking that has made Aubergine Wealth so incredibly rich.'

'Exactly,' said Mordonna. 'Well, I have cousins in Mongolia: Surge and Alexeye. We can send word for them to watch the airport for when they arrive.'

Once they realise we are going to Mongolia, Chrysanthemum wrote, *I expect they will have spies waiting at the airport.*

Of course they will, Aubergine wrote back.

---

[51] *Of course, in some countries, the kings and queens do have to make sacrifices to get the job. In Britain, for example, they have to have their ears stretched so they stick out a really long way and have their chins removed and talk with a really stupid accent. (See* The Dragons 1: Camelot *for more information about talking posh.)*

Probably Surge and Alexeye. They are Mordonna's cousins. They run a yak kebab shop and are incredibly stupid.

Because he firmly believed in the famous statement Knowledge is Power – to which he added the footnote And Power is Money – Aubergine Wealth always made sure he knew as much about everyone as he possibly could. The details that he knew about every single one of the students and teaching staff at Quicklime College and all of the Floods and a million other people were staggering.[52]

He not only knew that Mordonna had two distant cousins in Mongolia and that they owned The Jolly Gulag Yak Kebab Shoppe, but he also knew how many pairs of socks each of them owned and what colour they were. He knew that Surge was allergic to thistles and had an inside leg measurement of eighty-seven centimetres on his left leg, but only eighty-five centimetres on his right leg, which meant that when he got drunk on Old Kremlin Ale, he always walked

---

[52] *See the back of this book for some little-known Floods facts.*

143

round in circles until he tripped over himself.

He knew that Alexeye was married to the All Mongolian Heavyweight Wrestling Champion, Tattyana Khan, who was a direct descendent of Ghengis Khan and owned two-and-a-half pairs of socks, all a dark shade of grey. Most of the information Aubergine had stored in his head and on three massive computers was completely useless, but you never knew when some little detail might make all the difference between ending up with fifteen cents or fifteen million dollars.

So as the plane lumbered towards Ulan Bator, which his computers told him was home to thirty-eight per cent of the Mongolian population, twenty per cent of whom lived on less than $1.25 per day, Aubergine sifted through Surge and Alexeye's details to see if there was anything that might be to his advantage.

There was.

It turned out the two brothers had their very own illegal yak farm right up in the far north of the country. It was hidden deep in thick pine forest in the second largest land-locked country in the world.[53] Because the two brothers were wizards, albeit not great wizards like their Floods cousins, they were powerful enough to create illegal six-legged yaks. As everyone knows, the leg is the tastiest bit of the yak and absolutely the best part for making yak kebabs.

---

[53] *Aubergine made a mental note not to buy a boat while they were there.*

We will go to their yak farm, Aubergine wrote to his wife, *and transplant Winchflat's bug into one of their six-legged freaks and we will then take it across the Russian border and set it free in the most massively huge, mind-numbingly, boringly repetitive pine forest in the world where it will never be seen again.*

Is there any way you could make copies of the tracking bug? Chrysanthemum wrote back. *If there is, we could put one in the yak, another in an eagle and one in each of the Kebab brothers.*

Brilliant! Aubergine wrote, falling in love with Chrysanthemum yet again, which meant he was now in love with his wife three times at once.

He could just make out the slight bump the bug made underneath his lead head shield. He concentrated, summoning all his magic powers, and focused on the bump. He could feel it wriggling under his skin and suddenly there were two of them. He focused again and then there were four. He hoped that Winchflat would just think the distance the bug was transmitting over was causing some sort of shadow and not suspect that anyone had actually cloned the device.

Sure, he is the cleverest wizard in the family of cleverest wizards, Aubergine thought, *but he just thinks he's so clever that no one else would ever be able to copy any of his wonderful devices.*

Sure enough, when the plane landed in Ulan Bator, one of the few places on earth that sounds as if it's been spelt backwards, the two Floods cousins were waiting. Surge and Alexeye had disguised themselves as each other – which, considering they were identical twins, was a bit pointless – and were dressed as Belgian tourists. This had been a really stupid thing to do because Mongolia gets so few visitors that anyone who does go there for a holiday is instantly surrounded by newspaper reporters, opticians who assume they must need glasses, a very small crowd of screaming children and a very large crowd of screaming sheep.

The chaos at the airport allowed Aubergine and Chrysanthemum to slip through Immigration virtually unnoticed, especially when Aubergine showed the officials his I-Am-From-An-International-Charity-That-Is-Thinking-Of-Giving-Your-Country-A-Huge-Amount-Of-Money-Card. Outside, the terminal was almost deserted apart from a three-legged yak tied to a broken-down old cart.

'Excuse me,' said Chrysanthemum to the yak driver, 'would you mind moving? You're standing in the taxi rank.'

'I am the taxi rank,' said the driver. 'Where do you want to go?'

'Take us to a nice, quiet hotel, please,' said Aubergine in a clear, steady voice so that Winchflat wouldn't miss a word.

'Hotel? What's that?'

'It's the place where visitors stay.'

'Ahh, you mean the pig sty,' said the yak driver. 'Bit of a problem there, I'm afraid.'

'Why is that, then?'

'Well, there is an international beetroot convention in town and all the beds are taken.'

'International?' said Aubergine.

'Indeed, sir, people have come from far and wide,' said the driver. 'Some as far as right down the end of the road past the big rock, and they are all wide.'

'Would this help?' said Aubergine, pressing a fifty-tugrik note into the driver's hand.[54]

'Oh my,' said the driver. 'So the rumours are true. There is such a thing as a fifty-tugrik note.'

'So can we get a room?' said Chrysanthemum.

'For such wealth I will sell you my house,' said the yak driver. 'My wife and fifteen children and I will move into my mother's cave. Well, I call it a cave. It's more of a hole in the roots of a big tree.'

'We only need it for a few days,' said Chrysanthemum. 'You can have it back then.'

The yak driver was speechless. He had been impressed when he had seen that the two visitors actually had all their teeth, but the idea that the two foreigners would pay fifty tugriks just to borrow his house for a few days was beyond belief.

When they have gone, he thought, *I will call the*

---

[54] *About four Australian cents.*

Guinness Book of Records (Mongolian Edition). *Though I doubt they will be believing such wealth and extravagance.*

'And when we leave,' Chrysanthemum added, 'we will give you two more fifties. One for your inconvenience and one to forget you ever saw us.'

This will probably get into the All of The Russias Edition, the yak driver thought before he fainted.

When he regained consciousness, he drove them to his house and led them inside. He loaded his wife and children onto the cart and took them away. Fifteen minutes later the yak came back, pushed the door open and went to sleep in the kitchen. The driver had explained that this might happen as the creature was a Homing Yak.

'But do not worry,' he said. 'He does not snore, though I would advise you to keep the windows open.'

A strange bit of advice as the house did not so much have windows as holes in the wall through which the cold Mongolian wind whistled a sad, plaintive air, a seriously-cold-thirty-degrees-below-freezing plaintive air that made the two travellers grateful for the soft clouds of warm steam coming from the piles of yak dung that covered the kitchen floor.

So we need to remove the four tracking bugs from your head, wrote Chrysanthemum.

Can you do that sort of thing? Aubergine wrote.

No problem, wrote Chrysanthemum. *I was in the Girl Guides.*

So Aubergine drank seven bottles of Old Kremlin Ale, including the lumps, and passed out.

When he came round he felt as if he had been kicked in the head by a yak, which he had because Chrysanthemum had done the operation on the kitchen table, right next to the sleeping yak, which was thrashing about in its sleep due to a nightmare involving a giant beetroot and a short-circuiting electric balalaika. Its thrashing had knocked the table over, which had hit Aubergine on the left side of his head, and then its flailing feet had hit him on the other side.

'All done, my darling,' said Chrysanthemum, wrapping Aubergine's head in a bandage and mopping up the blood. 'I've put the bugs inside the bandage so they will appear to be in the same place.'

Aubergine Wealth was not an electronics expert. In fact, he found torches rather confusing. However, as every five-year-old knows, it doesn't require much time or skill to build a wi-fi multi-channel transponding auto-tracking remote control, and in five minutes Aubergine had bodged together such a device out of a toilet roll tube, a bent hairpin and some lichen. The device allowed him to control which one of the four tracking bugs would be sending out a signal.[55] He then deactivated three of them. Of course, Aubergine could have simply destroyed the original bug, but he had always resented Winchflat's vastly superior brain and this way he could prove he was just as clever as any of the Floods.

Back at the airport, Mordonna's two distant cousins were clever enough to realise that spying on Aubergine by hiding behind a tree and watching him would not work.

'He will see us,' said Surge, who was the brain of the operation.

'This is true, brother,' said Alexeye, who left the difficult stuff like thinking to his brother. 'And we will see him.'

'We're supposed to, stupid, but he is not supposed to see us.'

'Oh.'

'But do not worry, for I have a foolproof plan,'

---

[55] *The hardest thing was finding a toilet roll tube. Mongolian toilet paper is actually a small hedgehog wrapped in rhubarb leaves.*

said Surge. 'I have tied a ball of red wool to the taxi. All we have to do is follow it and we will know where they have gone.'

Like all taxi drivers the world over, the yak man had taken a long and complicated route to reach his destination. He had taken so many turns and returns and fresh turns that the wool ran out right outside the kebab shop, long before he had delivered the travellers to his house. The wool had, however, woven itself into a rather nice bathmat.

That evening Aubergine and Chrysanthemum disguised themselves as two peasant girls by rubbing yak dung in their hair and wrapping their feet in wet

Hello boys.
Fancy a
beetroot?

felt and went to The Jolly Gulag Yak Kebab Shoppe just as the two brothers were closing up for the night.

'Hello, boys,' Chrysanthemum said in a Mongolian peasant flirty voice that sounded like a rabbit being dragged through sharp gravel. 'Fancy a beetroot?'

She waved a bunch of beetroots at the brothers and lured them into a dark alley, where Aubergine was waiting to greet them with unconsciousness caused by a bang on the head with a gigantic world-record-winning beetroot he'd stolen from the international beetroot convention down the road.

It only took a moment to implant the tracking bugs into their skulls and when they came round a few hours later, they assumed it had been the sight of the world's largest beetroot that had made them faint.

The eagle wasn't quite so easy. For a start, eagles don't like beetroots,[56] but they do like rats, and as there were more rats in Ulan Bator than beetroots it didn't

---

[56] *Except for the Scottish Golden Beet Eagle, though that actually prefers artichokes.*

take long to catch a couple. However, attracting an eagle's attention is quite difficult. You can't just wave a rat in the air and shout, 'Here birdy, birdy.'

Oh look, a human waving a rat about, the eagle will think. *Now what shall I do, fly down and try and get it, or simply grab one of the ninety-six other rats I can see that haven't got a human attached to them?*

Difficult choice, it will think. *NOT.*

As luck would have it, however, there was one rather stupid and very shortsighted eagle floating above the town that day. It was very hungry on account of not being able to see the ninety-six rats running around below it, but it could see one rat that appeared to be waving at it.

Ooh, dinner, thought the eagle and swooped down.

Yum, yum, get off, ouch, yum yum, nice rat, it thought in that order as Aubergine grabbed its leg, Chrysanthemum tied the bug to its other leg then Aubergine stuffed the rat in its open beak.

Then they gave the taxi driver not one, not

two, but three fifty-tugrik notes[57] and the three of them set off for Surge and Alexeye's secret six-legged yak farm, making sure before they set off that the bug tied to Aubergine's head was the only one that was activated. It was a slow journey because the taxi

---

[57] *Twelve cents.*

driver kept taking the three notes out of his pocket and counting them, and every time he did, he fainted with happiness.

'We will go and hide out in the ever-so-vast endless pine forests of Russia,' Aubergine said in a nice clear voice so Winchflat would catch every word. 'No one will look for us there and if they do, it is so vast and endless they will never find us.'

'Tell them we will work our way east until we reach the coast where we will settle down to enjoy our vast wealth,' said Chrysanthemum.[58]

'What's that, my darling?' Aubergine continued. 'You would like to live in a small village on the far eastern coast of Russia? I would like that too.'

'The money, mention the money,' said Chrysanthemum.

'With all this enormous wealth to carry, our journey may be slow, but just think, when we reach our destination we will probably be the richest people for five thousand miles.'

---

[58] *Remember – Winchflat can hear everything Aubergine speaks, but nothing anyone else says.*

'Brilliant,' said Chrysanthemum, falling in love with Aubergine again, so they were now in love with each other a total of five times with an average of two and a half times each.

'We will dine on caviar and champagne and that will just be breakfast,' said Winchflat.

When they reached the yak farm, they captured the biggest strongest six-legged yak, implanted the fourth bug under his skin and led him away to the Russian border.

Ooh, that's a big forest, the yak thought to himself. *I bet it's full of thousands of girl yaks and nice tender grass to eat and lovely sparkling mountain streams to drink from.*

When they got back to Ulan Bator, Aubergine gave the taxi driver a sedative before handing him their remaining Mongolian money, which included several legendary one-hundred-tugrik notes.[59] The

---

[59] *Eight cents. I keep reminding you of the Australian to Mongolian exchange rates because I'm assuming that many of you are as rubbish at maths as I am. So for the last time – four Australian cents is about the same as fifty Mongolian tugriks.*

total value of tugriks they gave the taxi driver was more than fifty-seven Australian dollars, enough to buy a small place in the country called All Of It.

Even though Winchflat was now tracking the yak and not Aubergine any more, the two runaways were still cautious. Rather than go directly to Transylvania Waters they flew via several places to Monte Carlo, where they spent a happy week fraudulently winning lots of millions at the Casino until they were politely asked to leave. The authorities knew they must be doing something illegal to keep on winning over and over again, but no matter how hard they tried, they could not work out what it was they were doing.[60]

---

[60] *I know, but I'm not telling you. I might go on holiday there myself one day and want to use the same system.*

161

'I know Aubergine Wealth said they were going east to the coast,' said Winchflat, 'but they are going in the opposite direction.'

'Maybe they've discovered the tracking bug,' said Mordonna, 'and they're trying to throw us off the scent.'

'It's possible, but I think it's unlikely,' said Winchflat. 'We all know Mr Wealth is one of the greatest geniuses ever when it comes to money and all that sort of stuff, but I happen to know he's useless with electronics. I gave him a torch once and he needed a user guide before he could turn it on.'

'Maybe his girlfriend found it,' said Mordonna.

'And be very careful before you make your next statement.'

She knew that Winchflat thought girls and computery stuff should not be, could not be and hardly ever were in the same place at the same time. Just to make sure he didn't say so, she clicked her fingers and all the red knobs on his control panels turned blue and all the blue ones also turned blue. Winchflat got the point.

'There's something wrong,' he said. 'They were travelling west through the Russian forests making strange grunting noises and now they are lying in a gutter in Ulan Bator with a hangover and seeing double.'

Aubergine had switched the yak tracker off and both the Flood cousins on. He counted to fifty, then switched them back.

'No, it's all right,' said Winchflat. 'Must have been some electrical interference.'

Then Aubergine did the same with the eagle tracker for fifty seconds.

'It'll make Winchflat think there's some technical problem with his equipment,' he said as he switched between the cousins, the eagle and yak again.

'What did you just do, Mother?' said Winchflat staring at all the blue knobs. 'My machine's gone haywire.'

'I just changed the colour of the knobs. That's all.'

'Well, something's not right,' said Winchflat, more than a little annoyed.[61]

'Maybe it's gone wrong,' Betty suggested.

'My machines never go wrong,' said Winchflat. 'I mean, they've all got secondary backup systems and special robot self-repairing thingies with spare screwdrivers and gaffer tape. They simply cannot go wrong.'

He buried his head in his hands. 'But I think it has,' he added.

---

[61] *Which for Winchflat means just a tiny little bit annoyed.*

'Have you tried re-booting the whole system?' Ffiona suggested.

'Both boots and fresh socks too,' said Winchflat. 'But it's still telling me that one minute Mr Wealth is heading west through the Russian forest, then a minute later he's seeing double in a Mongolian gutter before tearing a rat to pieces in a small pet shop on the edge of Ulan Bator.'

Aubergine Wealth switched back the yak and left it at that.

'It's OK,' said Winchflat with a sigh of relief. 'It seems to have stabilised. Must have been electrical interference. I've built filters in to allow for that, but there must have been a really big solar flare or something. They are still travelling west through Russia and it looks as if they heading towards Kazakhstan.'

'What are they talking about?' said Mordonna. 'Maybe that'll give us a clue.'

'I think the audio has gone . faulty,' said Winchflat. 'Since the solar flare interfered with the signal the audio has sent nothing but strange grunting sounds. I fed the sound into my computer and it says

it's the noise of a yak eating grass. So I think we'll just have to rely on the GPS bit.'

'Unless it is a yak eating grass?' Betty suggested.

'Well, little sister, how on earth could it … Oh,' said Winchflat.

'Wait!' said Chrysanthemum. 'I know it was a brilliant plan and everything, but I think there's something we overlooked.'

'What?' Aubergine asked.

'Well, the Winchflat boy could hear you speak too, couldn't he?'

'Yes.'

'So now he can hear you impersonating a yak having its breakfast, can't he?'

'Damn!' cursed Aubergine and hit the mute button on his remote.

'Let's hope it's not too late,' said Chrysanthemum.

There was no way they could know. On the one

hand, having switched between the four bugs should have made Winchflat think his machine wasn't working properly, so he might think the audio was playing up too. On the other hand, Winchflat had programmed his brain to totally reject the possibility that anything he invented could ever go wrong and Aubergine suspected that Winchflat would have analysed the sounds and discovered they were genuine yak-having-lunch noises.

'I think the only thing to do is switch on all four devices at the same time,' said Winchflat, 'and head for Transylvania Waters as quickly as we can. I know a secret way into Castle Twilight and once we get inside, there are hundreds of derelict and deserted rooms where we can hide for as long as we want. I mean, right under their noses is the last place they will ever think of looking.'[62]

---

[62] *Except for Satanella, who spent a lot of time in front of mirrors looking under her nose. Being a dog she had a highly sensitive sense of smell, and being hairy she got a lot of her dinner stuck round her mouth, so under her own nose was a very interesting and exciting place.*

'I was kind of hoping we could live in a little cottage by a stream in the country with a lovely old half-timbered barn full of safes where we could keep all our money,' said Chrysanthemum.

'And we will, my darling, but right now we need a safe haven where we can rest and plan our future,' said Aubergine.

So they got themselves some new disguises and joined a coach party of jolly Belgian tourists on holiday from the famous cabbage-pickling factories of Bruges. Two days later they arrived at the coach park by the entrance of the tunnel into Transylvania Waters. The tunnel had been deliberately made too narrow to allow anything larger than a medium-sized car to go down it, but as luck would have it, there was a huge fleet of Valla's Executive Taxi Cabs waiting to take the tourists through the tunnel into paradise and on to their hotel.

12

When the taxis arrived at the hotel, Aubergine and Chrysanthemum slipped quietly away into the woods behind the building. Aubergine Wealth knew the forests of Transylvania Waters like the back of his hand. In fact, he actually had a map of them tattooed on the back of his hand. Whenever he grew homesick as he had travelled the world, all he had to do was look at his hands and he felt happy again.[63]

---

[63] *The back of his other hand was tattooed with a map showing all the public toilets in Transylvania Waters. There was only one, so it was a very small map. He had maps and diagrams tattooed behind both knees and the soles of his feet were also tattooed: the left with a selection of Transylvania Waters's favourite insects and the right with an index to remind him which tattoo was*

The Wealths were an old Transylvanian family who could trace their ancestors to the very first settlers who had set up the country. They were one of the original Ten Families who had created the enchanted country to escape the Knights Intolerant, who had organised a world-wide persecution of witches and wizards in the very-long-time-ago century.

As a boy, Aubergine had scoured the forests with a metal detector searching for lost money. He knew every twist and turn, every cave and secret place there was to know, and he also knew a shortcut to Castle Twilight.

Up in his laboratory, Winchflat was going crazy. According to his sensors, Aubergine Wealth was in four places at the same time.

'And only one of them can be the right one,' he

---

where on his body, including the one with the security codes to his safety deposit boxes, which were on a very secret part of his body.

complained, twiddling all the knobs on the console.

'Or none of them,' Betty suggested.

'I'd guess that Betty's right,' said Ffiona. 'I'd guess that Mr Wealth and his wife discovered your tracking device and somehow made three copies of it and then put them, plus the original one, into four other life forms while they got clean away with all their money.'

'Girls, please,' said Winchflat. 'Might I suggest you go and play with your Barbie dolls and leave all the technical stuff to people who are experts.'

'Oh yes,' said Betty. 'So where are they, clever-clogs?'

'They're in Kazakhstan heading towards Uzbekistan,' said Winchflat.

'And this one?' said Betty, pointing at one of the screens. 'They are crashing round in a small pet shop eating mice.'

'And this one?' said Festival. 'They seem to have photocopied themselves and are both lying in ditches sleeping off hangovers.'

'Maybe they haven't photocopied themselves,'

Betty laughed. 'Maybe they're still drunk and are seeing double.'

Winchflat went bright red. Not only was he angry that his machine seemed to be broken, but he had to admit to himself – but not her – that Ffiona's suggestion sounded like the most likely explanation, which meant that he didn't have the faintest idea where Aubergine and his wife might be.

Oh God, he thought very quietly. *They could be anywhere.*

Which of course they were.

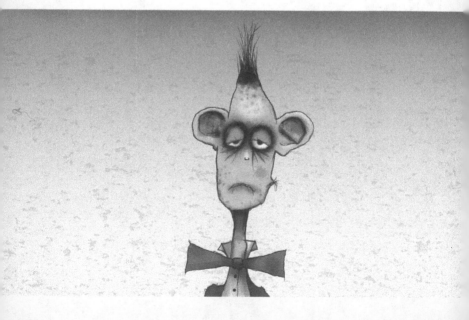

And the anywhere was much nearer than he would have ever thought.

'I think we must assume that they have outwitted you, darling,' said Mordonna.

'But . . .' Winchflat began.

It was the first time in his life that one of his inventions hadn't worked perfectly. Either they had outsmarted his tracking equipment or the equipment itself had broken down. Both options were unthinkable. Winchflat felt a great wave of depression sweep over him. His wife, Maldegard, put her arm round his shoulder, but there was no consoling him.

'I am not programmed to fail,' he said.

'None of us are perfect, darling,' said Maldegard.

'Except the Grand Master Wizard,' said Betty.[64]

---

[64] *Who may or may not be real.*

174

Meanwhile, Aubergine and Chrysanthemum were strolling peacefully through the forest towards the castle. Exquisite Scarlet Vampire Butterflies[65] fluttered around them and the air was filled with the delicate scent of deadly nightshade, which is always in full flower in Transylvania Waters. They each invited a butterfly to bite them and then drifted along singing old hippy songs.

Aubergine made an unusual hippy. His love for the finer things in life – money, more money and lots of money – was too deeply embedded in his soul

---

[65] *The Scarlet Vampire Butterfly is a strange and wonderful creature. First of all, it is the only butterfly that lives on blood, and second, it is the only creature that people queue up to get bitten by, because in exchange for a tiny drop of blood the butterfly injects them with an equal amount of its own dribble, which contains a chemical that turns them into a floaty happy hippy for the rest of the day. Some people actually keep a Scarlet Vampire Butterfly as a pet and have a little bite before they get up each morning. This, of course, is completely different from the Purple Vampire Butterfly, which makes you feel really, really Belgian for the rest of the day. If you are already Belgian then it makes you feel Welsh. If you are at all colourblind you are advised to avoid the forests of Transylvania Waters where these insects live.*

175

for a mere butterfly bite to override. Every fibre of his being was devoted to wealth, more wealth and lots of wealth. His blood was gold-coloured and his sweat smelled of crisp new banknotes, the smell that had first captured Chrysanthemum's heart.

They came to the end of the footpath through the forest and there was a tall stone wall. They were at the back of Castle Twilight – not just the back, but the unfashionable part of it, where the whole place was shrouded in permanent semi-darkness cast by the huge towers at the back of the castle. Aubergine took Chrysanthemum's hand and led her along the wall until they came to a small door that was hidden behind a curtain of poison ivy.

'My great-grandmother planted that,' said Aubergine, 'to hide the only entrance into the castle grounds apart from the main gate. I think one of my cousins still comes here to feed it and make sure it is still covering the door.'

'Doesn't it give you a terrible rash if you touch it?' Chrysanthemum asked.

'Yes,' said Aubergine and, reaching into his

176

pocket, he pulled out a silver spray bottle. 'Unless you cover yourself with my great-grandmother's special spray.'

They covered themselves. Aubergine unlocked the door and they crept into the gardens that surrounded the castle.

'Follow me,' said Aubergine, 'and whatever you do, don't eat anything. Those beautiful flowers over there may look like chocolate. They may smell like chocolate and they may appear to be waving their petals at you inviting you to eat them, but one tiny nibble and you will turn instantly into a Belgian accountant with a really bad limp and an enormous purple and yellow boil throbbing on your neck. Within an hour the boil will have grown seven times bigger than your head and then it will burst and you will be drowned in a flood of your own pus.'

Chrysanthemum looked as if she was going to throw up.[66]

'Though of course,' Aubergine continued, 'if

---

[66] *So did my editor.*

you were a Belgian accountant with a really bad limp you'd probably be quite relieved to be drowned.'

There were other equally terrible plants. There was the Ferocious Weaving Grass, which could grab you by the ankle and weave you into a basket full of very old herrings, and there was the Very Naughty Prickle Bush, which does such unmentionable things to its victims that they are unmentionable.

By picking their way carefully through the garden they finally reached the back wall of the castle itself. The wall towered above them, vanishing in places into the thick white clouds. The whole place had a really sad, depressing atmosphere about it, as if time itself had given up here and moved on to somewhere else.

'Can we get out of here?' said Chrysanthemum. 'I feel myself becoming really sad and depressed.'

'Don't worry, my darling,' said Aubergine. 'It's just a spell my wonderful great-grandmother put here to keep people away. Once we go inside the castle the spell will lift. You might still be really sad and depressed, but it will be a different really sad and

depressed and it will be for quite different reasons.'

Aubergine walked along the huge wall for a few moments, pausing now and then to slip his finger into a gap between the stones. Finally he stopped, pushed his whole hand into a gap and pushed. A large stone slid aside, revealing a small stone staircase.

They were inside Castle Twilight, right under the noses of the Floods themselves. Of all the places in the world they could have run to, this was the closest they could have been to their pursuers.

Almost.

'Come on,' said Aubergine, taking Chrysanthemum's hand and leading her through the darkness up the narrow stairs.

The stairs went round and round up in a spiral until they could go no higher. There was a heavy wooden door in front of them with a tiny beam of light shining into the darkness through a keyhole.

'Here we are,' Aubergine said as he pushed the door open. 'Perfect safety.'

But instead of the room Aubergine was expecting – the old, dark, deserted room with its treasure chests and simple oak furniture lit only by a single narrow slit in the masonry of the far wall – they found themselves in a bright white space bathed in sunlight.

Nor was the room deserted.

Aubergine Wealth was dumbfounded. His family had created their secret route in and out of Castle Twilight, the hidden gate in the outer wall, the secret stone into the castle itself with the spiral staircase leading up into the castle attics and then a long corridor to the secret tower, and in all that time they had never shared the secret with anyone outside their family. The Wealths had used the route and the hidden sanctuary for generations. Whenever there had been any financial hanky-panky in Transylvania Waters, a Wealth had usually been involved, and their hideaway right in the heart of the castle had saved their skin on quite a few occasions. He couldn't speak for any of his relations, but Aubergine Wealth hadn't been up to their sanctuary for a long time, certainly not since the

Floods had reclaimed the throne.

The person who was sitting in the red armchair in the middle of the room was not one of his relations.

'I thought you'd come here, Auby One,' said Mordonna, using her childhood nickname for him and also making a really bad *Star Wars* pun.[67]

Aubergine was speechless.

'Aren't you going to introduce me to your wife?' Mordonna continued as Aubergine struggled for words.

Aubergine Wealth and Mordonna had known each other since childhood. Because of their incredible skill in being very rich, the Wealth family – who gave their name to the state of being very rich – had been one of the few old Transylvania Waters families that Mordonna's evil father had not persecuted. In fact, they had thrived under his rule, a rule that had tended to overlook a lot of fairly illegal things that were now being dealt with by King Nerlin Flood and his counsellors.

---

[67] *Which as we all know is not possible because ALL puns are good puns.*

'Are you going to turn us in?' said Aubergine.

'Turn you in? Turn you in to what?' Mordonna laughed. 'No, no, no old friend, but I am going to put you out of your misery.'

'What misery?' said Aubergine nervously. 'In the past few months, I've made several billion dollars and fallen in love and got married. The first thing I took for granted, of course. Making fortunes is my natural talent. It's genetic, all my ancestors did it. The second thing was totally unexpected and more wonderful that I could have ever imagined.'

'More wonderful than the billions?' said Mordonna.

'Yes,' said Aubergine without a second thought.

Oh bugger, was his second thought when he realised that although he would have said the right thing in his wife's eyes, and probably in Mordonna's too, it might not have been strictly true.

'Did you really think you could outwit all of us?' Mordonna began. 'I know you were very clever, the way you kept throwing my dear Winchflat off the scent, but it was all irrelevant.'

'How?'

'We have known each other since we were children, haven't we?' said Mordonna.

Aubergine nodded and began to look worried.

Mordonna had spent her childhood locked away in Castle Twilight. Her father had kept her a virtual prisoner, imprisoned in a tiny castle with a mere two hundred and seventy-six rooms and a minute seventy-three-acre garden to play in. Her only friends had been the castle rats and a caterpillar called Brian, who had changed into a butterfly and deserted her, and the young Aubergine Wealth who, unknown to the king, had befriended the lonely princess.

'So I think you'll agree that we know each other pretty well, don't we?'

Aubergine nodded again and looked worried again and again and then some more.

'In fact, I'd say I probably know you better than you know yourself,' said Mordonna. 'Being as how I know lots of stuff about emotions and feelings and you know more about money type things.'

Aubergine stopped nodding. He just stood staring at his feet while Chrysanthemum held his hand and took over the looking nervous bit.

'What I mean,' Mordonna explained, 'is that for all of Winchflat's wonderful devices and all your clever subterfuges I knew all along that you would eventually end up here.'

'But even I didn't know that,' said Aubergine. 'I mean, I hadn't planned to. We just sort of made our escape up as we went along.'

'No you didn't,' said Mordonna. 'You were always going to end up in your family's secret hideaway. I was extremely surprised when you suddenly fell in love and got a wife. That really threw me. I had always assumed that if you ever did get married it would be to a very big cash register. I did have a small Plan B on hand in case you didn't come here, but thankfully it wasn't needed.'

Aubergine knew better than to ask Mordonna what her Plan B was. He had painful childhood memories of being confined in very small electrically powered boxes with very sharp bits when he had refused to share his lollies with her.

'So what are you going to do?' Aubergine asked. 'Do we have to give all the money back?'

'Oh yes,' said Mordonna, 'that and more.'

'More? How much more?'

'Well, you know the money you've hidden away that absolutely no one knows about?' Mordonna began.

Aubergine's mouth hung open as his thoughts raced round the world visiting all the secret stashes he had made over the years. As he realised later, this was about the worst thing he could have done, because Mordonna was one of the greatest mind readers of all time. Not only could she read his mind as it went from cache to cache, she could note them down in her head and locate them all to within five centimetres with her built-in GPS.

'Well, I say no one knows about it.' Mordonna smiled. 'Guess what?'

Aubergine Wealth collapsed onto a chair and buried his head in his hands.

Mordonna pressed a button and the middle of the room gently floated down into the room below, where Winchflat was making a few final adjustments to his massive Toilet-Roll-Magnet-With-Kitchen-Roll-And-Tissue-Attachments-Machine which was now an Every-Single-Cent-Aubergine-Wealth-Has-Magnet.

'Would you like to press the button?' Mordonna

asked Aubergine. 'Kind of say a personal goodbye?'

Aubergine did a goldfish impersonation, which meant he stood there with his mouth opening and closing and no sound coming out, just a few bubbles.

Chrysanthemum, who hadn't married him for his money, but had fallen deeply in love with it very soon after, shrugged her shoulders.

Oh well, she thought, *easy come, easy go.*

Not my lovely husband, she added in case anyone was reading her mind – which of course Mordonna was. *I just mean the money.*

Then something rather wonderful and touchy-feely and all hippyish happened. Mordonna, one of the world's most powerful witches, clicked her fingers and Aubergine Wealth was overcome with a powerful desire for a Tofu Burger with Bean Sprouts and Homeopathic Mayonnaise. He yearned to have flowers in his hair and move to the country and float over fields of buttercups eating strawberries covered in carob chocolate substitute. Chrysanthemum's recent conversion to the Wonderful World of Wealth faded away and she was re-overwhelmed by a love of pink things and soft faux-fur cuddliness. She could see the two of them growing broccoli and radishes together in a little cottage by a beautiful lake while a large number of once sad, lost and lonely puppies scampered playfully in the soft grass biting the heads off tiny lizards, but without the lizard bit.

Chrysanthemum, who never went anywhere without a bunch of flowers, wove them into her husband's hair and, holding hands, they pressed the button together.

All over the world Aubergine's soon-to-be-ex-fortune began to move.[68] The three hundred cardboard boxes under Aubergine's bed emptied. So did the enormous sock inside the plastic bag under the rock on Inaccessible Island that was guarded by a flock of really bad-tempered Rockhopper Penguins who spent all day hopping on and off the rock and spitting at anyone who ever went near it – which

---

[68] *Apart from the radioactive bit buried in the heart of the Chernobyl nuclear reactor. Winchflat had included a Dangerous Filter in the magnet so that stayed where it was.*

189

no one did so wasting all their spit made them even more bad-tempered. The rock actually rolled down the beach into the sea, which made the Rockhoppers really, really angry because they didn't have a rock to hop onto anymore.

'And hopping on tiny seashells just doesn't do it,' said the chief penguin.

Relieved of its contents, the massive wallet that that had been sinking into the lawn behind Aubergine's house lay there in the rain feeling that its life had suddenly lost all meaning. Not only had all the money it had been holding gone, but so had the credit cards and even the ten-per-cent-off seniors card for the Zurich Cash'n'Carry. All that was left was a photograph of Aubergine's tortoise, Bullion, and that had been chewed by ants.

All the wallpaper disappeared from the walls of Aubergine's house and six Swiss banks filed for bankruptcy. Every last cent everywhere, even the silver threepenny bits that Aubergine's mother had always put in the Christmas pudding each year, had gone from their tin in the larder, and all the

seventeen billion dollars that Aubergine had coaxed away from the population of New York was quietly returned to its previous owners.[69]

Aubergine was penniless.[70]

And he had never felt happier.

Mordonna did the old Cinderella trick and turned a pumpkin into a little cottage on the shore of Lake Tarnish. There were roses round the door, organic broccoli growing in the back garden, six chickens who hated broccoli, an assortment of lost, lonely puppies who had been treated with the famous Transylvania Waters Stay A Little Puppy Forever spell and a book on how to teach yourself the banjo. This was very useful as Aubergine was suddenly overwhelmed with the desire to play hill-billy music. There were no books on how to teach yourself guitar

---

[69] *Apart from $12,465,977.25 that had belonged to a really bad-tempered old lady called Chlorine VanderVelde Rooschild who was so mean she even made her illegal immigrant slave servants recycle their own dinners. (Don't ask and don't think about it – you will just feel nauseated.)*

[70] *Where Aubergine's wealth had gone will remain a secret for the moment.*

191

because Chrysanthemum already knew. There was also a nursery and two prams because Mordonna knew things that Aubergine and his wife didn't.

The husband and wife moved into their cottage and lived happily ever after apart from a splinter Aubergine got in his big toe two years later.

'Well, my darlings,' said Mordonna as the whole Floods family and their friends sat on the tallest tower of Castle Twilight drinking warm bloody slurpies while the sun set over the mountains behind Lake Tarnish, 'I hope no one wants to be a billionaire? Now Mr Wealth has dropped out, there won't be any more economics classes at Quicklime's.'

'Oh well,' said Betty.

After all, being witches and wizards who could basically magic anything they wanted out of thin air, it was no big sacrifice.

Some Little Known Floods Facts and Secrets

Nerlin Flood has four knees. The second two are at the back of his legs though they have been known to creep up into his armpits during thunderstorms. They were given to him by a witch when Nerlin said he would bend over backwards to help a small kitten that was trapped inside a sandwich. Without the extra knees, he would not have been able to bend over backwards and the sandwich would have been eaten which would have been disastrous for kitty. Since then Nerlin has rescued thirty-seven kittens, four puppies and a small accountant who were also trapped inside sandwiches.

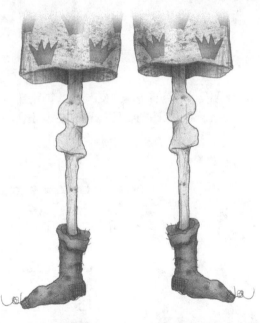

Betty Flood has a dark secret, but it is so dark that even with a really bright torch you can't see it.

Mordonna Flood collects cheese rinds. For many years she kept them in a special cabinet, but after she told her son Winchflat about the collection, he took it over and built a wonderful machine that converts the rinds into new and exciting life forms. These are set free to roam in Transylvania Waters's exciting new Wild Life Sanctuary where they have formed relationships with each other and produced newer and even more exciting life forms such as the duck-billed bank manager and the flying scalloposaurus.

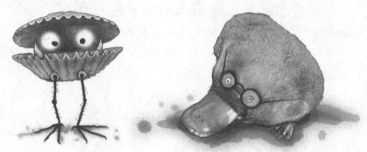

Late at night Winchflat goes to the Wild Life Sanctuary and seeks out his creations. Then he points at them and laughs.

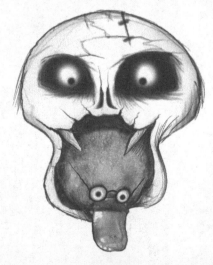

Late at night Valla goes to the Wild Life Sanctuary and seeks out Winchflat's creations. Then he creeps up behind them and sucks their blood, some of which is mauve.

DisGuys'N'Gals Boutique
Bad Taste is our Middle Name

HOTHEAD

Are you so hideous that you can only go out after dark? Wear this lovely bag. Now available in a choice of several male or female famous-but-forgotten-tomorrow TV legends.

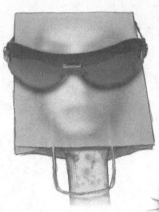

THE OGRE DRESS

Do people keep creeping up behind you and attacking you with soft fruit?

Well, you need the Ogre Dress and Matching Leggings. As they approach they will see this terrifyingly lifelike creature printed on your back and run away screaming.

They will probably drop their soft fruit and if it's a banana, they might even slip on it and break their necks which is no more than they deserve.

EDIBLE SOCKS

We've all heard of edible undies and yes, they are delicious, but nothing says I love you more than a pair of edible socks. These socks have been pre-worn for your dining pleasure by a Very Large Sumo Wrestler on a Very Hot Day. FREE toenail clippings with every pair. Enjoy.

Yum! Yum!

WARNING! ONLY to be used with adult supervision.

DANGER PANTS

Do people keep poking you in embarrassing places with soft fruit? Keep them away with Danger Pants – reinforced with real Barbed Wire and a pair of Genuine Eyes linked to your brain with wi-fi.

Now you won't be saying: 'Does my bum look big in this?'

You'll just say: 'Does my bum look?'

THE AMAZING COINCIDENCE ENGINE

The Daily News

CHICKEN IN MILLENNIUM SENSATION

AT the end of a quiet street, at the edge of a large town, stood a beautiful old house. The honeysuckle grew high around its walls and the paint curled up at the edges of the windows. Behind the dusty glass, dark velvet curtains brushed against a forest of cobwebs at the back of...

a tangle of fruit trees, a forgotten pond.

At the top of the... the traffic... by, but... short road to nowhere... peace...

Naked Chickens
• Page 8 •

Winchflat built the first version of this machine when he was three months old and actually designed it three months before he was born. Since then he has modified it and re-built it many times and it is now larger than a large house that includes a three-yak garage. Only part of it is shown here. The Octopus Untangler and the Soft Fruit Traumatiser are not shown as the patents are not sorted out yet and we wouldn't want any of you stealing the idea. In the meantime, of course, a lot of octopi are very tangled up.

Winchflat would like to point out that no coleslaw was harmed during the building of this machine, though a cabbage was sneered at a bit.

The Coincidence Machine works like this. You put a coin in slot A, plug the sensors into your ears, stand in a bucket of warm water and wait for a solar eclipse. At the very moment the sun is totally blocked out, your coin will drop out of slot B, but it will be (a) very shiny, (b) upside down and (c) sticky with the juice of soft fruit. If you then sit on the coin (clothing must be removed first) you will instantly understand Einstein's Theory of Relativity while looking a complete idiot and maybe even catching a cold, depending on the time of year you removed your clothing.

How to draw a ~~mask~~ mask on your face for a disguise

1. Take the top off your felt tip pen.
2. Go and buy *The Floods 1: Neighbours*.
3. Read it.
4. Go and buy *The Floods 2: Playschool*.
5. Read it.
6. Go and buy *The Floods 3: Home and Away*.
7. Read it.
8. Go and buy *The Floods 4: Survivor*.
9. Read it.
10. Repeat steps 3, 5, 7, 9.
11. Go and buy *The Floods 5: Prime Suspect*.
12. Read it.
13. Go and buy *The Floods 6: The Great Outdoors*.
14. Read it.

15. Go and buy *The Floods 7: Top Gear*.
16. Read it.
17. Go and buy *The Floods 8: Better Homes & Gardens*.
18. Read it.
19. Throw your felt tip pen away because it's all dried up.
20. Repeat steps 3, 5, 7, 9, 12, 14, 16, 18.
21. Forget what the pen was for so don't bother to buy another one.
22. Celebrate by buying *The Floods Family Files* picture book.
23. Eat some soft fruit.

DRAGONS 2
coming
OCTOBER 2010

FLOODS 10
coming
MARCH 2011